DEAD FLIP

Also by Sara Farizan

Here to Stay
Tell Me Again How a Crush Should Feel
If You Could Be Mine

DEAD FLIP

SARA FARIZAN

Algonquin 2022

Published by
Algonquin Young Readers
an imprint of Algonquin Books of Chapel Hill
Post Office Box 2225
Chapel Hill, North Carolina 27515-2225

a division of
Workman Publishing
225 Varick Street
New York, New York 10014

LIBRARY OF CONGRESS CATALOGING-IN-PUBLICATION DATA
Names: Farizan, Sara, author.
Title: Dead flip / Sara Farizan.
Description: First edition. | Chapel Hill, North Carolina :
Algonquin, 2022. | Audience: Ages 12–14. | Audience: Grades 7–9. |
Summary: "Eighteen-year-olds Cori and Maz, once inseparable best
friends, reunite to solve the mystery of what happened to their other
friend Sam—who disappeared five years ago and has now returned, not
having aged at all"—provided by publisher.
Identifiers: LCCN 2022013761 | ISBN 9781643750804 (hardcover) |
ISBN 9781643753324 (ebook)
Subjects: CYAC: Missing children—Fiction. | Friendship—Fiction. | Iranian
Americans—Fiction. | Lesbians—Fiction. | Massachusetts—History—20th
Century—Fiction. | Horror stories. | LCGFT: Novels. | Horror fiction.
Classification: LCC PZ7.F227135 De 2022 | DDC [Fic]—dc23
LC record available at https://lccn.loc.gov/2022013761

10 9 8 7 6 5 4 3 2 1
First Edition

To my sister Donna, who does not care much
for the music of the '80s but is the best thing
to have come out of the '90s.

DEAD FLIP

I.

MAZ

"THEY HAVE TO LEAVE SOMETIME," Derek said as we looked at the group of twelve-year-old boys surrounding *Street Fighter II* in the arcade near the mall's food court. They were cheering on a guy my age. Dude was taking his time trying to get his K.O. but I was fine with that. Derek didn't know that I preferred video games on home consoles or that arcades made me uneasy. He was my best friend, but there was a lot we didn't talk about.

"I think they're in it to win it," I said, mimicking Coach Gillis and punching at the air with my fist.

"Want to kill some time on original *Street Fighter*?" Derek asked.

I looked over toward the game, but I could only focus on the two pinball machines behind it, both neglected in the darkness. I took a deep breath and turned around. I had to get out. "Let's go to Sam Goody instead."

"Sure," Derek said. "I can't wait for *Insecticide* to come out." We turned into the bright light of the food court.

1

"Eh." I shrugged. "You can't party to Nirvana. Except for 'Smells Like Teen Spirit.' Then it's like you read the lyrics and it's such a bummer. Wreckx-n-Effect, now *that's* the future of music."

"That's what you said about Kris Kross."

"Yeah, because 'Jump' was genius!" I bounced up and down in front of Derek until I bumped into someone. "Sorry!" I turned around to find I'd gotten in the way of two young women.

One of them, an East Asian girl with streaks of pink in her black hair, combat boots, and a flannel tied around her waist, kept walking. The other stood dead in her tracks, staring at us. She looked a lot like my childhood crush, Tiffany. I blinked a few times before I realized who she was. "Cori. Um . . . hi." It was all I could manage.

"Hey, Maz," she said quietly. "It's been a while."

"Yeah." It had been five years. We hadn't even really said goodbye. We just stopped talking. Her brown hair, which she'd worn in pigtails when we were kids, was down around her shoulders. She was an inch or two taller than me, wearing a yellow summer dress and a denim jacket, and looked like a white girl right out of *Beverly Hills, 90210*.

The pink-haired girl doubled back and joined her.

"Looks like our friends have entered a staring contest," Derek joked to her. "I'm Derek."

"Janet," she replied.

I knew I had to say something to keep things breezy, but I couldn't do that with Cori. She'd see right through it.

"I'm Cori," she said, extending her hand out to Derek. "It's nice to meet a friend of Maziyar's." It was?

"Cori and I grew up together," I explained. "We used to be best friends." I don't know why I said that. It was as stupid as being freaked out by the arcade.

"Used to be?" Janet asked. I guess Cori had never mentioned me. To be fair, I'd never talked about her, either.

"People change." Cori's voice was cool and her friendly smile was a practiced fake. Cori may have transformed into a model, but I could still read all of her facial expressions. "How's the family?"

"Good, thanks," I said. "How about yours? How's Tiffany?"

She grinned—this one for real—and rolled her eyes. "Now how did I know you were going to ask about her?" I chuckled a little. I suppose my thing for her older sister hadn't been the well-kept secret I thought it was. "Everyone's fine," she continued. "Tiffany is still Tiffany. I'll tell her you said hello."

I saw her eyes dart around my face. Maybe she was doing the same thing I was. Noticing how much I'd changed and how much I'd stayed the same.

"How about we continue this reunion over an Orange Julius?" Derek suggested. Going to an all-boys school like Carter Prep made meeting girls an unmissable opportunity.

"I'm lactose intolerant," Janet said, folding her arms across her chest. "And Cori promised me a guy-free evening. Didn't you, Cori?"

I saw Cori blush a little. It was slight but totally there.

"No sweat. We've got stuff to do, too," I said. We hadn't hung out in five years. What was another five?

"It was good to see you, Maz," Cori said before Janet dragged her away.

I didn't call after her to tell her it'd been good to see her, too. There wasn't any point.

"Who doesn't like an Orange Julius?" Derek asked. He turned to me. "All good?"

"Yeah," I lied as I watched Cori walk away. She didn't look back.

2.

MAZ

"'WOLFMAN'S GOT NARDS!' That was the best line of any movie ever!" Sam shouted in the empty theater. There had been a couple in the back, but they'd left before the movie ended. More people should have appreciated *The Monster Squad* when it was in theaters. I guess they had cooler stuff to do, like drive their girlfriends to the mall. Tiffany's boyfriend, Brooks, was so lucky. He dressed like a preppie fool, but maybe that was what she liked. That and his car.

Next to me, Cori had her notebook out. She always liked to watch the credits with horror stuff and take notes on who did what.

"No way, the best line was when the little sister said, 'Come on, you guys, don't be chickenshit,'" I said.

Sam held up his hand for a high five. I slapped his hand, and we both grunted, "Buds." We thought we were so cool. What a couple of dorks. Sam's dad hadn't bothered to make him get a haircut all summer, and his shaggy brown bangs flopped in front of his giant green eyes.

"Are they explaining the whole plot of the movie in a rap?" Sam asked, as the credits rolled.

"Yup," I said, getting up. I lifted my shoes from the sticky floor.

"It's catchy." Sam bopped back and forth. Of course, Sam liked that dumb song. I hoped he wouldn't randomly rap it at school. I had already talked to him about the Melody Pops. He played the *Indiana Jones* theme song about five hundred times on the lollipop before I told him to cut it out. We couldn't do that baby stuff in seventh grade.

"There was a rap like this for *Fright Night*, too," Cori said as she continued to scribble down the names she saw on the screen. "It's patronizing."

"Oooh, big word, Cori," Sam said, pretending to be impressed. Cori and I had watched *Fright Night* on TV, but we didn't tell Sam because he didn't like scary movies. Even during *The Monster Squad*, he'd covered his eyes a couple of times and jumped up in his seat. I'd pretended I hadn't noticed.

Once the soundtrack credits came on, Cori closed her notebook. "Okay. We can go now," she said.

The monster movie master had spoken.

🎵 🎵 🎵

When we entered Rob's Newsstand, the smells of sugar, yellowing newspaper, and pickles from Rob's sandwich hit my nostrils.

"Well, if it isn't Moe, Larry, and Curly," Rob said from behind the glass counter full of expensive pipe tobacco, fancy

Zippo lighters, and political campaign memorabilia from the Roosevelt and Eisenhower years. Rob was a short, stocky white guy in his early sixties. His thinning hair was always messy, like he had just woken up from a nap. He wore huge eyeglasses that never drooped down his pug nose.

"Nyuk, nyuk, nyuk," Sam said, channeling Curly from the Three Stooges. "Man, Rob, it's so hot in here!"

"Hey, if you'd like to pay for AC along with all the comics you read but never buy, be my guest."

"How's it going?" I asked Rob.

"So long as Bill's buying scratchers, I'll keep afloat," Rob said, nodding at a scruffy, heavy-set man who was hunched over a small plastic lottery stand. Bill was there so much he felt like a part of the place, but that was my first time hearing his name.

We picked our candies. Pink lemonade Juice Bar gum for Cori, Melody Pop for Sam, and strawberry Bonkers for me. When we put them on the counter, Rob set his hand on the Melody Pop.

"No dice, kid. You can buy any other candy if you're going to be hanging around," Rob said. "Or I'll sell it to you on your way out."

"No one appreciates great art anymore," Sam grumbled.

"Aw, don't be sore, Curly," Rob said. "I've got a surprise for you kids."

"New comics?" Sam asked.

"I got something better than a comic book. Go take a look by the sodas."

The three of us walked to the back of the store, past the

cereal boxes and cans of soup. There, beside the clear fridge full of sodas, in all its electronic glory, was a pinball machine.

"All right!" Sam exclaimed, rushing toward it.

I sidled up to the machine next to Sam. The game was called *Sorcerer*. There were two dragons that mirrored each other with their mouths open, about to gobble the flippers up. The Sorcerer, with his long white beard, reached his hand up in the center; his hat—with yellow stars on it—cut between the point circles. Another sorcerer, with the same white beard but with horns, shot lightning out of his fingers. There were red lights shaped like eyes in the back of the playfield that weren't lit up. Yet.

It was a little old, kind of dinged up. There were pinball machines that were newer at the arcade, but the longer I looked at it, the more I wanted to play. I could see myself spending hours on it, waiting for the multicolored lights to shine and having my initials on the scoreboard for years to come, my legendary skills on display for all time.

"Pretty cool, huh, Cori?" Sam said.

"I guess," Cori said, unimpressed. She opened the fridge and took out a Tab for herself and a Mello Yello for Sam.

"I'm not thirsty," Sam said. I knew that probably wasn't true. Sam didn't have a steady allowance like Cori and I did. Cori opened the fridge to put the Mello Yello back.

"I'll get it for us to split later," I said. "It's hot out."

Sam smiled a little and turned his attention back to the machine.

"You like it?" Rob asked as he crept up from behind us, taking his place next to the scoreboard.

"It's boss!" Sam's fingers were already on the flipper buttons, ready to play.

"Would you believe I found this at an estate sale?"

"What's an estate sale?" I asked.

"Yard sale for dead people," Cori explained as she closed the fridge door.

"It had some broken glass, but it wasn't too hard to spruce up. It's practically as good as new." Rob sucked in his stomach and pushed his glasses up, even though he didn't need to. "Want to know something else?"

"What?" Sam asked, his eyes full of wonder.

Rob reached behind Sam's ear and produced a quarter. I saw Cori roll her eyes. Dumb magic tricks weren't her thing—she only liked them in movies.

"It used to belong to Mr. Davenport," Rob said, waiting for Sam to take the quarter from his fingers.

"Whoa," Sam said, still looking in awe at the coin. "Wait, who's Mr. Davenport?"

"The guy who lived in that mansion near Brooks's family," Cori cut in, her eyebrows raised. Cori liked anything spooky and the Davenport mansion fit the bill. "His family made a lot of money in textiles."

"What are textiles? Also, what would an old guy want with a pinball machine?" I asked. "No offense, Rob."

Rob laughed at this and flipped the coin in the air. I caught it. A strange rush of warmth came over me. I felt like I'd been picked first for basketball at recess. I handed the quarter to Sam. He was always picked last in everything.

"I'm not *that* old. Davenport was in his nineties when he finally passed. Most of us in town never thought he would." From the front of the store, Bill cleared his throat real loudly to get Rob's attention. He wasn't much of a talker. "Better sell Bill his smokes. Have fun, kids. You're the first to play it!"

"Yes!" Sam said. He shoved the quarter in the slot.

I could have sworn the START button lit up before the coin dropped. Sam pulled on the plunger and sent the silver ball up the lock ramp. When he did, the two fiery red eyes from the back of the board lit up and flashed. The Sorcerer said "Feel my power!" before the eyes flickered and the ball released. I tried to play it cool and not show my excitement, but Sam cheered.

"Vickie Greenfield called me," Cori said, handing me her soda. "She invited me to her house for a party Thursday afternoon."

"Really?" I asked. Cori got along okay with the girls in our grade, but she never really hung out with any of them outside of school.

"You're not going to go, are you?" Sam asked, his eyes still on the game.

"I told her I'd let her know if I could make it. She said you guys could come, too."

The ball slipped through Sam's clutches and rolled past the Shoot Again circle.

"Could be cool." I shrugged. Sam looked at me like I had said Schwarzenegger was better than Stallone. These days it might be all about Arnold, but back then, everyone with a clue knew Stallone was king. "I bet they'll have fancy snacks like shrimp cocktail."

"Is Nick the Dick going to be there?" Sam asked.

"Probably," Cori muttered. Sam and Nick didn't get along at all. I didn't remember how it had started back in fourth grade, but they were always butting heads, especially since Nick had started calling him Sam the Squirt. I played sports with Nick, but maybe I should have done a better job of being peacemaker. "She said she has a Nintendo."

"We're going, then," I said. My parents wouldn't get me one because they thought video games would rot my brain.

"Fine," Sam muttered. "She better have *Duck Hunt*."

I turned my attention back to the Sorcerer. Not as much attention as it was paying us. Before Sam pulled on the plunger for his second turn, I felt I was being watched. I looked at the machine. The painted red eyes in the back, the ones that would light up, moved. It was quick, but they flicked from me to Sam before they shifted back into place.

"Maz?" Cori put a hand on my shoulder. "What's up?"

I should have told her what I saw. Maybe it would have kept all of us together.

"Nothing," I said. I thought I was probably dehydrated. I took a sip of soda and watched Sam play until it was time to go home.

3.

JANET LAY ON MY BED, studying her textbook. She couldn't see me studying her as I sat cross-legged in front of the headboard. I wasn't sure what to make of *us*. We were friends, but not at school. Janet's friends were what Vickie would call *alternative*. Janet called my social circle *pristine and mean*, which I didn't think was fair, but I understood the sentiment. Janet was the most incredible person I'd ever met. I hated that my stomach felt like a Chestburster would pop out of it whenever she was around.

"What did you get for question seven?"

"What?" I asked, sitting up too quickly.

Janet turned her head in my direction. "You seem preoccupied." She shifted on the bed to face me, brushing a pink strand of hair behind her ear. "Is it your friend we saw at the mall?"

I let out a deep breath. For now, I could avoid romantic land mines. Besides, it was better not to fantasize about a life that was impossible for someone as chicken as me to have.

"Right. Maz," I said, my body deflating into the pillows.

"You didn't say much after we bumped into him. Old boy-friend?" For someone who understood me so well, she hadn't picked up on the one major thing. "You don't have to talk about it if you don't want to. But if you do, I'm here."

Dammit, Janet. I really like you.

There was a scratching at the door. With a slight prod, my Yorkshire terrier, Potato Chip, let himself in. I got PC from a shelter when he was four. Tiffany said he looked like a poor man's Popple, so we named him after one of them. These days, he wasn't able to jump up onto the bed like he used to. Janet scooped PC up and plopped him between the two of us, his slobbering tongue and heavy panting breaking the tension.

"Hi, buddy," I said, giving his head a pat.

"Potato Chip, how'd you get so handsome?" Janet asked as she wrapped her arms around him and held him to her chest. I had never been jealous of my dog before, but, well, this was a low that a homecoming queen nominee should never experience. "I hope I didn't overstep. Asking about your friend."

"No, it's . . . I've spent a lot of time *not* talking about Maz," I said, staring down at the comforter. "We were best friends since kindergarten. Until our other best friend, um—well, he went missing."

"Missing?"

"Yeah, um, our friend Sam Bennett—"

"Ghost Boy?" she blurted out, then immediately covered her mouth with her hand. "I'm sorry, I didn't mean—"

"It's okay," I lied again. "He built up quite the reputation." The local media circus had been relentless for about a month after Sam went missing. And because it happened while he was trick-or-treating, all the headlines played into parents' worst fears. It was a better ratings grab than a kid finding a razor blade in an apple. "Maz and I were obviously both really upset."

"No kidding. That's so horrible," Janet said. Her hand found its way to my knee. My breath hitched, and I closed my eyes, trying to contain myself. I hoped it looked like the memories were painful. They were, but if she knew how I felt about her, I wasn't sure she'd want to stay friends. I'd lost enough friends for a lifetime already.

"We were kids and didn't know how to cope. And I guess we both felt guilty because we were the last two people to see Sam." I opened my eyes but looked a little past her, to the *Edward Scissorhands* poster on my wall.

"It must have been so rough for both of you," she said. I nodded, because it was, but only Maziyar knew how I felt. "I would think that would bring you two closer?"

"It did at first," I said. "Until we had a big fight. I don't remember about what."

Another lie.

"He looked excited to see you," Janet said. "Maybe he wants to patch things up?"

"Maybe," I said. Only *I* didn't want to patch things up. I was glad to see Maz was doing well, but I was happier with every-thing behind me. "Would it be all right if we dropped it?"

Janet nodded, then cradled PC in her arms, treating my old dog like a baby. I was sure she had a million questions, but all she did was hum as she rocked him back and forth. I averted my eyes, looking back to the poster of Johnny Depp in white makeup holding Winona Ryder.

Janet followed my gaze and then turned back to my dog. "What do you think, Potato Chip?" she cooed. "Do you think Johnny is sexy, too?" The alien in my stomach chewed on my intestinal lining instead of popping out.

4.

CORI

"YOU MISSED A SPOT ON THE RIGHT," Tiffany said from her lounge chair as I pushed the reel mower over our front lawn. She hadn't taken her eyes away from her magazine once, but she somehow knew which patch of light yellow grass needed attention.

Mowing the lawn was supposed to be her responsibility, but when I asked Tiffany if she could drive us to Vickie's party, that favor came with some conditions. Her chores became mine.

She wore a pink bikini and a pair of black Wayfarer sunglasses that Brooks bought for her. Cars slowed down whenever Tiffany tanned in front of our house. I sometimes saw Maz look at her with puppy dog eyes. He hadn't done that when we were younger, but Sam explained to me that Tiffany had a "bodacious bod, even if she is a demon with a heart full of puke." He did have a way with words.

Tiffany was very pretty. She still is.

Boys appreciate that.

I get it.

But Maz wouldn't even admit that Tiffany was, at times, an asshole. He'd always make excuses for her, like "Maybe she just forgot to pick you up from the movies" or "She loves you. She only calls you an idiot sometimes because that's what older siblings do." That was a lie. Maz never called his baby sister, Nilou, any names other than *cutie pie* or *smushy face*.

"Come get something to drink," Tiffany said, lowering the volume a little on the radio. "I don't want you passing out. I'd get so much shit for it."

I pulled the collar of my shirt up to wipe the sweat off my nose (an unladylike habit I've since broken) and poured myself a Solo cup of Crystal Light and guzzled it down. The cup was left over from the party Tiffany threw the weekend my parents went to my uncle's place in Maine. I spent most of my time locked in my room reading *Carrie*, which wasn't so bad. Mom never quite knew what to do with my love of horror, but by the time I was twelve, she had become more accepting as long as I continued to get good grades, Just Said No to drugs, and didn't join a Dungeons & Dragons group that would lead me to a satanic cult. I think all of those very special sitcom episodes and evening news reports had more of an impact on her than she realized.

"While you're here . . ." Tiffany passed me a bottle of sunscreen. I already knew the drill. I put down my cup and sat on the edge of her chair. She turned her back to me. I squirted some lotion on my hand. The bottle made a farting noise. "Ugh," she said. "Why do you have to be gross at everything?"

"Sorry," I said. I wasn't, but I thought if I played nice, she'd leave me alone. Poor, sweet, naive baby Cori. I put the lotion on her shoulder and started rubbing it in, avoiding her high ponytail of raven hair. Her bangs were teased out and drenched in hairspray. To me, they looked like a giant claw jutting out of her forehead, waiting to catch unsuspecting boys in its clutches.

"Tell your nerd herd they better not be late," Tiffany said. I didn't tell Maz she called him and Sam that behind their backs. Sam wouldn't have cared. He had plenty of names for Tiffany himself. But I knew if Maz found out, he would mope around like a Romero zombie in a shopping mall.

"Okay."

"Don't forget my lower back," she said. I rolled my eyes because I knew she couldn't see me. "Which one of them do you like better? Sam or Maz?"

That was like asking which eye I wouldn't mind being gouged out. It had always been the three of us. I couldn't imagine it any other way.

"I like them both the same."

"One day you're probably going to have to choose one of them," she said with certainty as though she were telling me the earth was round. "Guys don't stay friends with girls. They don't know how once they see boobs and butts, which you're on your way to having."

I suddenly felt anxious. Not about Tiffany's warped hypothetical of having to choose one of them to date. I was worried because I didn't want to date anyone. Vickie Greenfield had liked Nick Dawson for forever. She went on and on about it at recess with her friends, but she never went up to Nick to tell him. If I had liked a boy, I would have told him. But I guess that's easy for me to say because there wasn't a boy I felt that way about. There still isn't, even though I sometimes wish there was.

"You have guy friends," I argued. Tiffany had no trouble surrounding herself with admirers.

"I wouldn't call them *friends*. They're just there to kill time with before I get the hell out of high school. One more year and then no more having to laugh when Brooks makes a stupid joke. He's so needy. I sometimes think he'd like me to applaud him when he ties his shoe or takes a piss."

"Why do you stay with Brooks then?" As soon as the words were out of my mouth, I tensed. Tiffany always controlled the conversation. She still does—when she bothers to call.

"You're not that young. You must have figured it out by now." She closed her magazine and put it on the lounge chair. Paulina Porizkova's face on the cover looked up at me. She had a knowing smirk, piercing blue eyes, and dangling earrings. She looked like she was going to eat whoever was taking her photograph. My mouth felt dry even after I downed all that Crystal Light.

Tiffany turned her head slightly, eyeing me. She flipped the magazine over. I felt embarrassed, like I'd been caught, but I didn't know why. Tiffany cleared her throat. Maybe she knew something about me that I hadn't quite figured out yet.

I put more sunscreen on her but she really didn't need it. I started lightly writing in cursive on Tiffany's back. I wrote *witch*, looked at it for a moment, then smeared the word into her skin.

We both turned when we heard "Is This Love." It blared from a car cruising down our street.

"I hate that song," Tiffany muttered. She shooed me away, put her hands under her head, and stuck her chest out like she was modeling for a swimwear ad. She didn't smile or wave. She looked up at the sun as a red Mustang GT pulled into our driveway.

The engine cut off, along with the music. Brooks Wallington exited his car wearing a green polo shirt tucked into white shorts. He took off his sunglasses and hung them on his collar, showing off his baby blues. Objectively, I understood that he was handsome. He had a sharp jawline; he was in shape; he kept his wavy brown hair short and slicked back. It never looked out of place. But seeing him in shorts, I couldn't get over how pasty his legs were even when they were covered in so much hair.

"Ladies," Brooks said as he walked over to us. "How's it going, Corinne?"

I wished he wouldn't call me Corinne. It's the name my parents use when I'm in trouble or visiting my grandparents at Easter.

"Fine," I said. "How are you?"

"I've got no complaints." Of course he didn't. His family had a fortune from building strip malls. "I didn't know you were going to be home."

This meant, *Scram so I can fool around with your sister.*

"Cori's helping me out with some housework." Tiffany hadn't even looked in Brooks's direction yet. "There are a lot of dishes in the sink that she needs to wash after she's done mowing the lawn. She might be here awhile."

"How about I do the dishes to speed things along?" Brooks offered. Did he know how to do the dishes? Didn't his family have maids or butlers to do that?

"Why, Brooks, that is so sweet of you," Tiffany said finally, flashing him a smile. "Maybe after I get dressed, we can go to the mall?"

"Sounds good, babe." Brooks crouched down to give Tiffany a kiss. She turned her head so he got all cheek.

"Not in front of Cori, sweetie," Tiffany said, putting her hand on Brooks's chest.

"Oh. Right." Brooks stood back up, blushing. "Sorry, Corinne."

Tiffany had kissed other boyfriends in front of me before. She was using me as an excuse so she didn't have to play what Maz would call *tonsil hockey* with Brooks in that moment.

"Let me get to those dishes," Brooks said, wiggling his fingers in the air before bounding into our house. Tiffany watched him, beaming, until he was out of sight. Then her face twisted into something wicked. I couldn't see her eyes, but her nostrils flared and her smile was all gritted teeth.

5.

"ALL RIGHT, FELLAS, BRING IT IN," Coach Gillis said.

The two sophomores on varsity cross country, Craig and Brewster, were doubled over and heaving. They weren't used to Coach's one-kilometer, two-kilometer intervals yet, but they should have been with all the summer training we did.

"I'm dying. This is it. This is how I go," Derek whispered to me in between gasps. "On the Carter Prep campus like a chump."

"You're going to live," I muttered back, lightly tapping his chest. Derek and I were co-captains, so we had to look like we enjoyed working hard. Derek liked the leadership role, but he didn't need this the way I did. He was a straight A student. I got solid Bs with the occasional C, which my parents hated. He was a senior prefect and a great baseball player in the spring. Cross country was *my* thing. I loved to run. It wasn't exactly the sport that alumni came to see, but it was getting me noticed by some universities and colleges, even ones out of state.

The best thing about Carter Prep was that it was in a different town, so people didn't look at me with worry like they had at Walnut Mills Middle School. Even if anyone at Carter remembered Sam's disappearance, they didn't know I had known him. I didn't have to go through high school as Ghost Boy's sad-sack friend.

"I see some of you enjoyed your summer break," Coach said as we huddled around him. Coach Gillis had also been my Algebra II teacher and helped me after class when he didn't have to. He wasn't a teacher who got picked to speak at graduation, nor was he ever asked to head up ski trips or sign kids' yearbooks. That was what I liked about him. At a school where anything less than perfect was unacceptable unless your parents donated a bunch of money, he managed to not get caught up in the crap. He treated everybody the same and wanted us all to run for him, even if we were far from being the best team in the league.

"We'll get them in shape, Coach," Derek said, before chugging half his water bottle.

"I'll hold you to that," Coach Gillis promised. His baseball cap shaded the top half of his face so I couldn't quite read his expression, but I think I might have seen a bit of a grin. "Wanted to remind you that our first team dinner is coming up next week. Paul's family is hosting."

"Dinner starts at seven," Paul said, wiping sweat off his forehead. "Please shower after practice that day." I think he was expecting us to chuckle or something, but most of the team was too out of breath to find much of anything funny. We all took turns hosting a team dinner before a race. Captains were supposed to host first, but I think Paul was still pissed the team didn't vote for him to be one. When Coach told us that he'd volunteered for the first dinner, Derek and I were happy to let him have it. The last thing the team needed was drama.

"There's also the matter of the middle school's Harvest Dance," Coach continued. All our dances were with the Nichols School, an all-girls prep school where my sister, Nilou, was a seventh grader. "They need chaperones. Now, I'd gladly volunteer, but well, my daughter, Cleo, is trying to make friends and she's expressed that my being there might be embarrassing."

I could see that. Nilou had also forbidden my parents from chaperoning anything.

"There are a few Nichols seniors who are going to be helping the teachers. I thought it'd be great if my seniors could do the same." All five of us seniors looked anywhere except at Coach. The field, the sky, the mud on our sneakers, so long as he didn't make eye contact with us and take it as volunteering.

"Something to think about," Coach said, in a way that let us know he was going to bring it up again. "Rest up and let's get in it to win it." He punched the air with his fist.

"All right, fellas! Hands in," I said, starting a huddle. The team—Quincy, Paul, Brewster, Craig, Derek, and Ezra—pathetically grunted, "Go Carter." This is where *my* version of leadership came in. "That will not stand, gentlemen!" I used my best 1950s-style radio voice and pointed my finger up toward the clouds. "We may be tired and we may not be ranked with the best of them, but gosh darn it, we will have school spirit!

To be without school spirit is un-American. Now, who do we represent?"

"Carter," the guys said a little louder, still panting but smiling.

"The school that taught us to be men! That taught us to be brave! That taught us our donations as alumni will in fact be tax deductible! Who are we?"

"Carter!" the group shouted.

"A little louder so I know you MEAN IT!" I shouted back.

"CARTER!"

"That's what I'm talking about," I said, dropping my voice back to normal. "Now was that so hard?" I patted the two sophomores on their backs and the rest of the team staggered off the field. All except for stupid Paul.

"See you tonight, Maz," Paul said, loud enough so Coach could hear. He said it with a mischievous grin that made him look constipated, then turned and headed off to the locker room.

"Tonight?" Coach asked.

Shit. Derek, who was now lying down on the grass and stretching, glared in Paul's direction and then stared at me in panic.

"We're going to hit up McDonald's, have a chicken-nugget eating contest," I lied. "Just a little team bonding."

Coach's lips were tightly pressed together. I guess I wasn't very convincing.

Carter Prep had a no-tolerance policy for drugs and alcohol that could result in expulsion. Last year, two juniors were asked to leave the school after being caught with flasks at a dance. The dummies. You didn't bring the party onto campus.

I put my arm around Coach's shoulder and stood by his side like we were old pals at our twenty-fifth high school reunion. He didn't move a muscle.

"Coach, I would never jeopardize the futures of our best and brightest," I said, pointing at me and then him. "We've worked too hard for that, haven't we?" Coach didn't answer. When he tutored me in Algebra II, he'd often say he felt I wasn't applying myself to my full potential. I never confirmed or denied that for him. "I promise there is nothing illicit about Chicken McNuggets. Unless they've started lacing sweet-and-sour sauce with something I don't know about." I let go of his shoulder and extended my hand out for him to shake. "I haven't let you down yet, have I?"

He gripped my hand, hard. "No, you haven't," Coach said, not letting go when I started to pull my hand away. "I expect you won't in your most important year, either."

I knew what he meant, but I hated the phrase. I didn't want to think that my senior year of high school was going to be my *most* important year. Who wants to peak at eighteen? Then again, I should be so lucky. Some people don't even get that far.

"I wouldn't dream of it, sir," I promised. I guess that was good enough for Coach because he finally let go. It must have been that *sir* at the end. Teachers love that shit.

"Have a safe weekend. See you Monday." And with that, he finally left the field.

"You sure about tonight?" Derek asked me as he tossed me his water bottle.

"Are you worried you won't be home in time for TGIF?" I said, squirting water in my mouth before tossing the bottle back to him. "It's a welcome-back get-together. Low-key, small crowd, everything's going to be copacetic." Derek didn't look so sure. "If you're not having a good time, you say the word and we're out of there. Of course, you could always stay home. I'll let the girls know you were busy."

He rolled his eyes and waved me off.

"I'll see you at eight," he said with a sigh. "Enjoy your 'fun run.'"

I grinned and headed off to the woods.

❧ ❧ ❧

The Carter campus ended at a pet cemetery. It was a part of our race course and I was used to running through it, but I guess it was kind of creepy. Summer was still in the air, but New England autumn was making itself known with gusts of wind that made my skin prickle. It used to be my favorite season.

Running helped me focus on my breathing, get out of my head, get so exhausted I didn't have energy to dwell on the past. It was also something I could do alone. I didn't have to be "on" all the time. The way I'd learned to be, so people wouldn't look at me with pity or concern. When I was running, I didn't have to pretend that I was okay. I didn't have to pretend that I thought Sam was dead, the way everybody else did.

For a while, after Sam was gone, I'd hear his voice in my head.

I think it did something, Maz. I think it wants me.

I ran harder. Trying to drown it all out again. But when I saw a ball of fur lying on its side by a giant oak tree, I slowed my pace. Maybe the pet cemetery staff accidentally misplaced someone's beloved guinea pig. I stopped jogging as I got a little closer and saw that it was a squirrel. I've seen dead squirrels before, especially on Route 128, when they've been crushed by a car and their guts are oozing out. This squirrel didn't look like mangled road kill. It wasn't curled in on itself like a limp, wet noodle. Its legs stuck straight out, like it'd been stuffed for a trophy room. There were flies hovering above, but they never landed. I guess they didn't know what to make of the little guy either.

I picked up a stick. I'm not a nature expert, but I hadn't ever heard of squirrels playing dead before. I kept my distance and poked at its back foot very gently, giving it a chance to run away if it wanted to. It didn't move.

I turned the squirrel around with the stick so that it was facing me. Its mouth was wide open, as though it was in mid-scream, if squirrels even screamed. I shivered when I looked at the bugged-out eyes staring at me. When one of the critter's eyelids twitched, I stumbled backward.

I heard a whistling among the trees.

It was soft, slow, and familiar. I turned to see where it was coming from but didn't see anything or anyone. I dropped the stick, backed away from Nutkin, and jogged back to school.

The whistling stopped. I tried to get it out of my head, but I couldn't. It sounded like the theme from *Indiana Jones*.

6.

MAZ

WHEN CORI SAID HER SISTER WAS GOING TO DRIVE US to Vickie's house, I didn't think we'd be squished in the back of Brooks's car. I didn't hate Brooks, but, man, was I envious of him. From the seat behind Tiffany, I could see her reflection in the passenger side mirror. Her sunglasses didn't do much to hide how annoyed she looked, but even pissed off, she was so beautiful. I had absolutely *no* chance, she kind of scared the crap out of me, and I couldn't really form words around her, but I tried to get as much face time with her as I could. Sometimes I'd practice what I'd say to her in my bathroom mirror, but whenever I tried it out in real life, I sounded so awkward. One time I asked her if she liked weather.

"You like this song, Brooks?" Sam asked from the middle seat. "It's kind of mushy."

I saw Tiffany smirk. I guess she thought the song was kind of mushy, too.

"Trust me, kid. When you get to be my age, you'll find women love this stuff. Right, babe?"

Not true. Women are complex, multifaceted individuals who like lots of different genres of music. Plus, hair metal is dead.

Tiffany didn't respond, but her smirk had gone bye-bye. Brooks put his hand on Tiffany's thigh. She continued to stare out the window. Then she looked directly into the passenger side mirror, pulled down her glasses, and winked at me. The yelp that came out of my mouth surprised all of us.

"You okay, Maz?" Cori asked.

"He's probably nervous because you're driving too fast, Brooks. Better to have both hands on the wheel," Tiffany said, no longer looking in the mirror. "There are babies on board."

Brooks listened and put his hand back. That was the power of Tiffany. She could have asked me to rob Fort Knox for her and I would have. I didn't like that she called us *babies*, but I guess we were. Nobody warns you what a trip twelve is. Thirteen gets all the attention, but twelve is chock-full of hang-ups and pressure.

"I guess I am going a little fast," Brooks said. "Sorry guys."

"That's okay, Brooks!" Sam said cheerfully. "Tiffany's used to going fast."

"Sam, don't. Please," Cori whispered. He could have kept his mouth shut. We were four streets from Vickie's house.

The sappy song ended, but the cassette kept playing and another equally sappy song took its place. How did Tiffany stand this guy? I tried to study what it was about him she liked. He was a jock, had a great car, and I guess he was sort of carefree?

"Earth to Maz," Sam said, waving his hand in front of my face. "Where'd you go?"

"Nowhere." I looked back at the mirror. Tiffany was smirking at me. My stomach felt warm and funny. When I jerked my head away, I heard her laugh. She must have known I liked her. God, I was such a dweeb.

"What's so funny?" Brooks asked his girlfriend. *His* girlfriend.

"Just thinking about how nice it'll be when these three don't have to beg for rides to their little parties," Tiffany jabbed back. "I'm surprised Sam gets invited to any."

Sam started faking maniacal laughter. Cori and I exchanged looks of dread.

"You know what I remember, guys?" Sam asked in between laughs, gasping for air. "How we saw Tiffany making out with that guy Steve at the movies back in June? She told us not to say anything, remember that?"

Brooks stopped the car in the middle of the street. A driver behind us honked.

"Steve Oleander?" Brooks asked with disgust. "From shop class?"

"You know him?" Sam asked. "He seemed nice." I elbowed him, but he didn't stop. "Good taste in movies, too. We were shocked to see Tiffany at *Spaceballs*. She wouldn't know a good joke if it bit her in her butt."

Tiffany coolly turned her head toward us. Her wide eyes were focused entirely on Sam. For a kid who covered his eyes during scary movies, he was brave enough to lean into Tiffany's face.

"Get. Out." Tiffany seethed. Sam didn't flinch, but Cori did.

"He's kidding," Cori lied. We'd all seen it. I don't think Steve had a bike, never mind a cool car.

Then Tiffany turned to me. I couldn't breathe. She didn't shout at me, but I felt like her words could topple me over. "Open the door. Now."

The three of us spilled out of Brooks's car.

"You can find your own ride home," Tiffany yelled. Brooks drove off, his tires screeching.

I turned to Sam, my fists clenched and shoved into my pockets. "You had to open your big mouth."

"It's a nice day for a stroll," he said with a shrug. "Vickie's is only a few blocks away." Without even looking at us, he started to walk.

"You made things harder for Cori," I shouted. Sam turned around to look at Cori. She didn't say anything, but she let out a sigh and started walking toward Vickie's without us.

"See?" I told him.

"I didn't think Tiffany would get that upset."

He was so full of it.

❧ ❧ ❧

"It's time for spin the bottle!" Vickie shouted. I sat in the circle right away. I may have had a thing for Tiffany, but Jennifer and Becky were pretty cute, too. Jeez, overeager, much? Cori and Sam didn't join me. They stood by the snack table. Cori stared at the punch bowl as though she'd never seen red juice before. Sam was stuffing his face with chips. The snacks were plentiful, but not in the league of shrimp cocktail. That had been wishful thinking on my part. Vickie may have lived in a big house on a cul-de-sac, but her folks weren't going to spend appetizer money on a middle school party.

I didn't have too much competition in the kissing department that night. The only other guys in the circle were Nick and his lackeys, Adam and Tim. Nick was tall for our grade and great at sports. Adam had demonstrated at many school lunch hours that he could burp the entire alphabet. Tim wore a white sports coat with the sleeves rolled up and looked like he spent a little too much time watching *Miami Vice*. I shouldn't judge. I had used more hairspray and mousse for the party than anyone should, even in the eighties.

Vickie sat down across from Nick. She beamed at him, but he kept sneaking glances at Cori. He'd been doing that a lot, but Cori never seemed to notice. Nick and I got along most of the time, except when he went after Sam. I never asked Nick about why he picked on Sam, but I got the impression he was jealous of all the time Sam spent with Cori.

"Okay, who wants to spin?" Vickie asked. None of us made a sound. "Come on! It's no big deal."

"Why don't you go first then, Vickie?" Jennifer offered.

"Cori," Nick yelled. "Want to spin?" Everyone turned to look at Cori. I saw her shoulders tense a little.

"No, thanks," she said.

"I can spin first," I said. I didn't really want to, but I wanted Nick to leave Cori alone.

He ignored me completely. "You're going to hang out with the Squirt all afternoon?" he asked. Sam licked chip dust off his fingers. I kept telling Sam not to let the nickname get to him. So he was short, big deal! I wasn't much taller. Sam's dad always said he was short at twelve and then had a giant growth spurt, and Sam probably would, too. Mr. Bennett was six foot one.

"Forget about them," Vickie said, her back to Cori and Sam. "Sam's not even supposed to be here anyway." Her voice was casual, like she was talking about what she had for lunch.

"Let's go," Cori said to Sam before she looked in my direction. "We're leaving, Maz."

I began to stand up, but Nick got to his feet first and put a hand on my shoulder.

"You don't have to leave," Nick said to her. "The Squirt is welcome to play, too." Jennifer made a gagging noise. I can't believe I thought she was cute.

Sam straightened up and puffed his chest out, like the wrestlers we watched on TV.

"No can do. These lips right here"—Sam pointed to his mouth and channeled Ric Flair—"are reserved for Elisabeth Shue and girls that don't have Pringles stuck in their braces."

Jennifer covered her mouth with her hands.

"Like Elisabeth Shue would even breathe the same air as you," Vickie said.

Sam just smirked. "I forgot. My lips are also reserved for Nick's mom."

That's when Nick grabbed Sam by the shirt. I rushed over.

"He didn't mean it," I lied, trying to get myself between Nick and Sam. I put my hand on Nick's wrist, trying to get him to loosen his grip.

"Tell him to behave, Maz," Nick growled. Sam was trying to keep that dumb smirk on his face, but his eyes were wide and there was a little sweat by his ears.

"He will. We promise. Right, Sam?" I glared at him.

"Sure," Sam mumbled. "Sorry, Nick."

"Please let him go," Cori asked. Nick gazed at her for what felt like way too long. She blushed. "Please?"

Nick released Sam and went back to the circle. He sat with his back to us and spun the bottle.

"Maybe this was a mistake," Cori whispered to me.

"Why? We were having fun before, weren't we?" I asked. Sam headed to the punch bowl. I didn't think he needed more sugar, but I wasn't his babysitter either.

"*You* were having fun." Cori said it like an accusation, but wasn't that what we were supposed to do at a party?

"This whole thing was your idea! You're the one who wanted to come."

"Nick got Vickie!" Becky squealed from the circle.

I couldn't see Vickie's face, but I bet she was grinning from ear to ear. That's what that whole party was about, wasn't it? Getting to kiss Nick. It's probably why she invited Cori in the first place. Cori was the best bait for Nick Dawson.

"Okay, whatever," Nick said. He leaned into the circle, waiting for Vickie to meet him. I watched frozen in horror as Sam toddled over to them, carrying the punch bowl.

Right as their lips were about to meet, Sam shouted "Pucker up!" and dumped the punch on both of them. Nick and Vickie were drenched in Red Dye 40. Sam dropped the bowl and turned to Cori and me. "Run!"

The three of us zipped up the stairs from Vickie's basement. We tore through her kitchen and out the front door, her mom's "What's wrong?" mixed with Nick's yelling after us.

❧ ❧ ❧

"We're right behind you," I gasp-yelled. Our running had morphed into sad jogging. Sam was faster than us, and he stopped on the sidewalk and laughed as he waited for us to catch up to him.

"Did you see the look on Nick the Dick's face?" he asked.

"I saw the look on Vickie's face," Cori said, her cheeks scarlet red and her nostrils flared. "That was juvenile, Sam."

"We are *juveniles*, Cori. Jeez, lighten up. You didn't want to play their stupid game anyway." Sam was still giggling as he wiped sweat off his nose. Cori didn't argue with him.

"We're not too far from Rob's," I said. "We can call our parents from there."

"Hanging out at Rob's is way better anyway," he agreed.

"Was that your plan, Sam?" I rounded on him. "Ruin the day so we'd spend it doing the same crap we always do?"

"Since when is the *stuff* we do crap?" Sam asked, his voice suddenly quiet and cracking a little.

"We can't keep goofing around just the three of us.

We're going to have to get along with other people, you know?"

"You want to trade us in for Nick and Vickie?" Sam asked with a scoff. He looked at Cori, waiting for her to back him up. She didn't.

"I don't want to trade anything," I said. "But you can't act like that and force us to deal with the blowback. Everyone is mad at us now. Nick, Vickie, Tiffany—"

"What do you want me to do, Maz? Get out of your life so you can hang out with creeps and fakers?"

"I want you to grow up!" I instantly regretted it. Sam's shoulders dropped.

"There's nothing great about growing up, Maz," Sam muttered, kicking at some loose gravel.

He walked ahead of us. I was about to join him when Cori took me by the arm.

"Go easy on him," she whispered.

"We're always easy on him!" I was louder than she wanted me to be. She gripped my arm a little harder.

"He was waiting to tell you . . ." Cori said. She paused to make sure Sam was out of earshot. "He's moving."

"What?"

"His dad told him two days ago. They're headed to Florida in January."

"Why did he tell you and not me?"

She slipped her hand down to mine and squeezed it. "He's afraid to. You're his best friend," she said.

"So are you," I said. "He likes you better."

"Obviously. I'm magnificent," Cori said with a straight face. Then she stuck her tongue out at me. I shook my head and squeezed her hand before letting go. "Come on. He's gotten too far ahead already." She was right. We couldn't see him.

❧ ❧ ❧

The lights were on at Rob's, and the store didn't close for another hour, but Rob himself wasn't in his usual spot by the register. The radio played a little louder than usual. I could hear the humming of the fan. I also heard the sound effects from the pinball machine. Sam had beat us there.

"Hey, Rob!" I yelled. This did the trick. I heard a flush. Half a minute later, Rob emerged from the bathroom customers weren't supposed to know about, but which he let us use when we were absolutely desperate.

"Hey yourself, Moe! No need to shout. Hi, Larry." Rob walked toward us. "Curly's in the back. He wasn't in much of a talking mood."

"Sorry," Cori said. "We were hoping we could use your phone to call our parents."

"No problem." Rob sat behind the counter, handing her the receiver of the phone he kept next to the register. I headed down the aisle to find Sam.

The *Sorcerer* machine was all ablaze, beeping and buzzing as Sam stood in front of it, his hands on the buttons. He didn't even bother to turn around as I approached.

"Sam, I'm sorry about what I said," I began, talking to the

back of his head while the numbers on the scoreboard went up. "Cori, she, um—she told me about Florida."

He didn't turn around or even acknowledge he heard me. Moving away from home is tough. I came to the US with my parents when I was four. I don't remember much of our old life in Iran, but I do remember crying a lot when I had to say goodbye to my grandparents. I love living here, and so do my parents, but I know how much they miss everyone we left behind. Florida was at least in the same country, but at twelve it might as well have been another universe. My bike could only take me so far.

"Florida's going to be cool! You'll never have to shovel snow." Sam wasn't buying it. His focus stayed on the stupid game. "And, hey, I've never been to Disney World. I know you've always wanted to go. I could come down there one day and we'll see if it really is the happiest place on Earth or if Mickey is full of it."

Even the idea of visiting the jewel of Orlando wasn't snapping Sam out of his funk. He had a row of eight quarters lined up on the playfield glass, but I didn't want to do this all night.

"I mean, is the move really for sure? Maybe we can work on changing your dad's mind?" I asked, standing beside him. I looked at the ball whizzing all around, hitting bumpers and point circles. "Wow, you're really good!"

Then I realized Sam wasn't moving his fingers. I looked up at his face.

No matter how hard I try, and believe me, I have tried for years, I can't get this image out of my head.

His eyes were rolled up so high in their sockets, I could only see white. His mouth was open, drool dripping down from the corners of his lips. Sam's usually pink skin was gray, his cheeks were caved in, and there were wrinkles forming on his forehead. Bluish veins bulged out of his neck like they were going to burst out of him.

"Sam!" I yelled, but he couldn't hear me.

The Sorcerer declared "Feel my power" as the ball kept bouncing off flippers that Sam had no control over. I shoved Sam hard. His hands let go of the game as he fell to the floor. I crouched above him. His eyes returned to their normal place. He blinked a few times, then stared at me like nothing had happened.

"What's wrong?" Cori rushed toward us, with Rob right behind her.

"It's Sam, he's—" I started, but Sam looked at me like I was the one who had a problem.

"I'm what?" he asked. "How'd I get on the floor?" He wiped spittle from his mouth with the back of his hand.

"Your eyes were weird, and your skin was crinkly . . . The game was playing by itself." I turned my head to look at *Sorcerer*. The scoreboard read GAME OVER. Sam's impossibly high score was wiped.

"Really?" Sam asked. I helped him up. "I mean, I was playing while I waited for you guys, but my eyes feel fine. Do my eyes look weird?" Sam asked Cori. She shook her head.

"Come on, guys, no roughhousing in here," Rob said. "You break it, you buy it. Understand?"

"You okay?" I asked Sam.

"Yeah, Maz," Sam promised. "You can let go of me anytime."

I did but my hands shook.

"You feeling all right, Moe?" Rob asked.

"Me?" I scoffed. "I'm fine!" Sam and Rob looked at me in disbelief. I turned to look at Sam. "I mean, I think. We should get you to a doctor or something."

"For what?" Sam laughed. "Because I fell?"

"I pushed you, actually," I said, realizing how dumb I sounded.

"You sure *you* don't need to see a doctor?" Sam asked. I knew what I had seen, but he was being a jerk about it, so I let it go.

"Well, if you kids are all set, I'd like to call it a day," Rob said, retreating back to the register.

"My dad's coming to get us," Cori said. "Maybe we'd better wait outside."

7.

CORI

IT SHOULD HAVE BEEN COOL TO BE NOMINATED FOR homecoming queen, but it wasn't something I ever dreamed about. Though I did strangely want to win. It would drive Tiffany up a wall. Despite her popularity, she never even got nominated. Vickie using her position on dance committee to intimidate junior and sophomore girls to hang up posters of me was kind of fun, even though it was weird. It was a little unnerving to have my smiling face plastered all over the school hallways, but a nice change from the tattered posters of missing people in our town over the years. Most people didn't seem to notice how many people had disappeared since we lost Sam, but I guess missing adults don't garner as much attention as lost kids.

"Your Majesty." Vickie was already at my locker.

"Hey, girlfriend!" I had rehearsed ways to sound upbeat over the years. My freshman year, there were times where it sounded forced, but now I could break into it without really trying. That didn't mean I didn't hate myself every time I did it.

"What are you wearing to the pep rally? I was thinking a little out of the box. What do you think of a bucket hat with a big sunflower on it?" I knew she wasn't going to wear that. Vickie played things safe. That was one of the few things we had in common.

"That could be cool," I said as I opened my locker. I had photos of Jason Priestley and River Phoenix taped inside. I understood that they were both very dreamy.

"I'd ask you to come over and try outfits on, but I don't know if you'll be able to pencil me in. You were *so* busy all summer."

"I was working," I said, grabbing my AP European History book.

"Can't kids figure out how to finger-paint on their own?"

"The art at camp was a little more involved than that." I kept my voice cheerful. I'd survived Tiffany. Vickie's passive aggressiveness was like kindergarten.

"I didn't even know you liked art. Are you going to show me your work sometime?" This was a definite no. If Vickie took one look at the monsters and horror art I came up with, I thought she would tell everyone I was a bloodthirsty hellion who had no place being homecoming queen and should be treated like some demon-worshipping outcast for all eternity.

An arm wrapped around my waist, pulling me away from my locker. I shrieked.

"It's just me, babe," Nick whispered. His hot breath on my skin made me squirm.

I turned around to face him, resting my hand on his chest.

"You startled me," I said, feeling Vickie watching us. Dating Nick was a recent development, one I had been putting off for years. He leaned in to give me a kiss on the lips, but I moved my head just in time so it landed on my cheek instead. I'd learned that trick from the best.

"You ready for the pep rally?" Nick asked. His eyes were bright. They always lit up when he saw me, and his smile was so goofy whenever he got close. I wish I could have returned an ounce of it back to him. He was a good guy. A little rough around the edges and kind of a jerk when we were kids, but he'd matured. "The team is running out onto the field to 'Enter Sandman.' It'll be sick."

Somewhat matured.

"That should be fun." I forced a smile onto my face. I wanted Nick to have everything he wanted. Except for me.

"Walk you to class?" he asked.

"We'd love that," Vickie answered for me, handing Nick her books.

I closed my locker and linked arms with Nick. A little farther down the hallway, I saw a head of pink-and-black hair. The hair, and the girl it belonged to, eventually walked by us without ever looking in my direction. I pretended not to notice, but she made that incredibly difficult.

❧ ❧ ❧

I smiled politely at a few art students in the hallway before heading into the darkroom. I couldn't see anything right away, but the sounds of k.d. lang's "Constant Craving" played from a boom box, so I knew she was in there.

"This song again?" I asked, trying to find her.

"If you don't like it, why'd you put it on my mix tape?"

I didn't have an answer.

"Don't worry. Nobody else is in here." Eventually, my eyes adjusted to the dark, the amber-colored safelight making everything look like a hazy dream. Janet leaned over a tray, her back to me as she poked at her print with a pair of tongs.

"I like it," I said, moving next to her. "It's just kind of . . . melancholy."

"I'm a melancholy kind of gal. I thought we had that in common?"

I looked down at the black-and-white photograph she was developing. It was from this summer, one of our campers, Zoe, wearing my zombie makeup while she stalked the woods, her face falling apart, latex flesh hanging off of her cheeks.

"Wow," I breathed. I had seen my makeup modeled before, including on Janet, but mostly in Polaroids. Never totally in focus or in a lush setting like a forest. It looked like a frame from a movie.

"Eerie, isn't it? I promised Zoe I'd send her a print. She's going to be so stoked."

The chemicals from the tray were assaulting my nostrils, but I couldn't stop staring at the photograph. Janet *loved* talking about cinematography in horror films, she knew who Rick Baker and Tom Savini were, and she had invited me to a Universal Monsters retrospective at a theater an hour away. She even drove us and paid for snacks that I liked and she didn't. She was perfect, even if she was wrong about Junior Mints.

"You're so talented," I murmured.

"Another thing we have in common," she said. This time, I could hear softness in her voice. "You did that, you know. You made that adorable kid a monster. It's a gift and you should do something with it. It'd be a shame if you didn't."

I wanted Janet.

I wanted her more than anything.

But I couldn't have her.

Even royalty had its limitations.

8.

CORI

AUGUST 20, 1987

"YOU WANT TO TELL ME WHAT REALLY HAPPENED?"
Dad asked as soon as we dropped Maz and Sam off at Maz's
house. I fidgeted in the passenger seat.

"We decided to leave early," I said, which wasn't a lie, but
Dad kept the car in park. Dad was the only Toyota salesman
who still drove his old Ford to work. We weren't going to go
anywhere until I told him the whole truth. "Some juice was
spilled in the heat of the moment. We felt it was a good idea to
leave the party before things got . . . juicier."

"Let me guess, Sam had something to do with it?" I didn't say
but we both knew. Dad sighed. "Did it spill on anything expensive?"

"Mostly on Vickie," I said. He didn't have to worry about
us needing to replace anything, except maybe Vickie's outfit.
Dad nodded, put the car into drive, and headed in the opposite
direction of our house.

"You're going to ring the doorbell, apologize to the
Greenfields, and offer to help clean up," he said. "You can't run

away from your problems. Only cowards do that. I didn't raise a coward."

"It wasn't my fault!" I objected, but lowered my volume when I saw Dad cock an eyebrow at me. "I mean, shouldn't Sam be the one apologizing? Does it have to be me?"

"If the company you keep does boneheaded things on your watch, then, yeah," Dad said. "Maz is a bright kid. I'm sure once he tells his parents about tonight, they'll set him straight. They're good people, for Arabs." I winced but didn't say that they were Persian not Arab or even that his comment was racist. "Maz's family works hard, they raised their kids to be polite, and you can tell they're going to turn out right. Sam? Jeez. He never had a fighting chance with a father like that."

I liked Dave Bennett a lot, but in the way one might like a funny older brother or an uncle who visited on holidays. Mr. Bennett became a dad at eighteen. I could tell he cared about Sam, but I could also tell he wasn't sure how to take care of him. He smelled like beer all the time, sometimes from being out after work (when he had work) and sometimes because Sam would get him a can from the fridge as soon as he walked into their apartment.

"Tiffany has got a good group of friends," Dad said. I didn't tell him she could barely stand any of them. "Brooks Wallington comes from a good family. A kind of family that—"

"Is very rich?" I interjected, more sarcastically than I should have.

"Has a good reputation," Dad continued. "It wouldn't hurt you to branch out a little. Make friends who can get through a party without property damage. Maybe even make friends with girls your age. Soon you'll probably want to talk to them about things you can't with Maz and Sam."

I wanted to push and ask him what things, but my parents were making their position clearer those days. Dad stopped asking me to go fishing with him. Mom kept leaving dresses on my bed. My tomboy days were supposed to come to an end.

❧ ❧ ❧

"Jennifer will . . . live in a shack, drive a Mercedes, have eight kids, and marry Phil the janitor." Vickie read out yet another MASH result. After I apologized to the Greenfields and Vickie, they asked if I'd like to join the girls for a sleepover. I was about to politely decline when my dad answered that I would love to and he'd go get my things and drop them off. There I was, listening to everyone laugh at Jennifer's supposed future, bored out of my mind and unsure of what to say. I knew it wasn't a crowd I could talk to about *Gremlins* or *Creepshow*. I also knew to laugh when everyone else did.

I sat on the couch with Vickie while Jennifer and Becky were on the carpet, the faded juice stain taunting me. I felt so lonely there. Everyone was nice, they hadn't done anything wrong, but I couldn't wait to go home.

"Let's do Cori next!" Jennifer exclaimed.

"Oh, that's okay," I said. Picking boys for me to live with in a mansion, an apartment, a shack, or a house was the absolute last thing I wanted to do. If I had been with Sam and Maz, we'd have been playing flashlight tag or listening to Springsteen or debating who was the coolest Ghostbuster.

"How about we watch a movie?" I asked.

"That comes later, silly," Vickie explained. Everyone else nodded. All of Vickie's fans deferred to her. I know now they had different personalities, but that night, they seemed like pod people. *Stepford Wives: The Middle School Years.*

"Okay, give us types of cars." Jennifer's pen was poised against a notepad as though she were a journalist about to interview President Reagan.

"Um . . . a station wagon," I said, struggling to come up with something.

"Forget the cars!" Becky said. "Give us guy names."

"Yes, Cori. Give us guy names," Vickie echoed. Becky and Jennifer's voices were high-pitched and excited when they spoke. But Vickie was calm, observant, and curious in a way that made me uncomfortable. She still gets like that sometimes.

"Um, Michael J. Fox," I said. Jennifer cheered, so I guess he was a good choice. "Corey Haim." He was great in *The Lost Boys.*

Becky dreamily murmured, "You'd be the Cories!"

"They can't all be celebrities," Vickie said. "You have to pick some real people, too."

"Celebrities are real people!" Becky protested. "I took a quiz in *Bop* magazine to see if Ralph Macchio was the right guy for me, and he was! If I ever met him, I feel like we'd really get each other."

"What about Nick?" Vickie asked, staring at me so intently it reminded me of Bela Lugosi in *Dracula.* "Would you put him on your list?" This was definitely a test. I had to be careful. I wanted to say what Sam would—"Gross. Cooties"—but I didn't want to insult her. I knew she wanted Nick all to herself. A part of me thinks she still does.

"He's not my type," I said with a shrug. Her gaze didn't leave me, but her mouth relaxed a little.

"Is Maz your type?" Vickie asked. This question made me tense. Tiffany had warned me about this, but I'd thought I had more time. I was behind my peers on that front. Quelle surprise. Everyone would notice if I didn't catch up soon. *There's the monster girl! She wants to marry the Wolfman!* To be clear, I do *not* think any of the movie monsters are sexy.

"Maz is like my brother, but if Ralph Macchio went to our school . . ." I said, wiggling my eyebrows the way Tiffany would when she talked to her friends. This got the girls to laugh. Even Vickie chuckled.

The phone rang. Becky ran over and picked it up as though it were her house, twirling the cord between her fingers.

"Hello! Tim?" she asked hopefully. Was this the part of the party where they got phone calls from boys? I wondered how it worked. Did they tell all the boys they were going to be at Vickie's house, then wait to see who called? Her shoulders slumped. "Oh. It's you. Hi."

"Is it Nick?" Vickie jumped out of her seat.

"I'll put her on. One sec." Becky put her hand over the receiver. "Cori, the Squirt's on the phone for you."

Jennifer cooed and made kissing noises. I got off the couch and took the phone from Becky, feeling my cheeks burning.

"Sam, this had better be an emergency," I said, turning my back on the party.

"I called your house and your mom said you were at Vickie's?" Sam's voice was full of disbelief. "A slumber party? Why are you doing that to yourself?"

"This is not the best time," I whispered into the receiver.

"Sorry. I'm calling from Maz's. But don't tell him I called you, okay?"

"Okay." He didn't say anything for a while. The kissing noises behind me got louder and louder.

"I've been thinking about what Maz said I looked like. At Rob's. And now I, um, I feel like something's not right."

"Tell Dr. S. if you're not feeling well." I was concerned but also annoyed. Never in the whole time we'd been friends had Sam used Maz's phone to call me, so this had to be important. Still, he was embarrassing me.

"He's still at the hospital and it's not that. I don't feel sick. I just feel like, um . . ."

"What?" I asked.

"Like I'm not alone," Sam whispered. "It's like someone's with me."

"Ask him if he wants to be on your MASH list," Jennifer shouted. I wanted to rip her braces off her teeth.

"I'm not kidding you," Sam said. "You gotta believe me because if you don't—"

Vickie yanked the phone out of my hand. I reached for it, but she turned away, blocking me.

"Sam. This is Vickie. You know this is a girls-only party. Don't you have any other friends you can call?" The girls all giggled. I grabbed the phone cord and pulled. Vickie dropped the receiver, letting it dangle in midair.

"Sam? It's me," I said.

"I think this is a bad time," he said. It was, but he was worrying me even more.

"Are you going to be okay?" I asked.

"Yeah. Aren't I always?" No. He wasn't. Even when he tried to prove to Maz and me that he was. "Bye."

"Bye," I said to a dial tone.

"What did the Squirt want?" Becky asked.

"Don't. Call. Him. That." I sounded so much like Tiffany that it scared me a little. The girls were all quiet. I glanced over at Vickie. She smirked, impressed. "So?" I asked. "When is pizza?"

"Can we order from Papa Gino's?" Becky asked.

"No! Domino's!" Jennifer begged. "No weird toppings like last time."

"Green peppers are not a weird topping." Becky rolled her eyes.

"Mom already placed the order," Vickie told her minions. "Cheese pizzas. From Pizza Hut."

They couldn't argue.

"I love Pizza Hut," I said. "Great choice, Vickie."

She linked her arm with mine. "I make great choices all the time." She practically strutted back to the couch. "Tonight, we are going to watch *Sixteen Candles* because Jake Ryan is boss."

"Is he ever," Becky agreed. "Such a hunk!"

I sat back down on the couch and listened to them chat about everything and nothing at the same time. It was almost like a game. Who could talk the most without actually saying anything revealing? It was a game I would learn to play. Quickly.

9.

SEPTEMBER 11, 1992

STACEY PAPADAKIS STARED AT ME, her face drawn in disappointment. It was a face I knew. She had given me the look many times over the course of our brief romantic relationship. The first was when she was telling me some nice childhood birthday memory and she asked me to tell her one of mine. I lied and said nothing came to mind. The second time was when she invited me to spend a week with her family at their summer place on the Cape and I said I couldn't come, even though she knew I didn't have plans. I didn't want to go. I wanted things to stay casual. I didn't want to get attached. The third time was when she broke up with me, a few days later, because she said she felt I always kept her at a distance.

She was staring at me, lips pursed and arms folded. "Are you worried about the cleanup?" I asked.

Her eyes darted to the guys from the Armstead football team shotgunning Narragansett cans in her garage. Girls from the Granger School field hockey team looked on, disgusted by the sight as they passed a flask among themselves.

"You said this was going to be a small get-together," Stacey hissed. There were more people here than either of us expected. Around fifty, and growing, by the looks of it. It was kind of a who's who of the senior jocks of private schools.

"Word got around." I shrugged. "But listen, I want you to be able to have a good time. Nobody's going upstairs and all the keys are accounted for." I showed her a cardboard beer box full of car keys. "We'll have this place sparkling clean before your parents come home on Monday. I promise," I said, giving her my most reassuring smile. She wasn't having it.

"I can't take you seriously when you're wearing that," she said, pointing at my hat. It was an oversize pirate hat that had a stuffed parrot attached to the brim. My teammates had bestowed it on me on our first day of senior year. I took it off as Stacey reached forward and gently removed my sunglasses. "What happens if my neighbors call the police? Do you have a plan for that?"

She had to be kidding. Her house was in a neighborhood where you had more chance of running into a deer at night than a cop car.

"I'll have Paul talk to them," I said. She gave me my sunglasses back, and I took the opportunity to hold her hand. She didn't pull it away. "You look gorgeous as always, by the way."

"No duh," she said, flipping her black hair with her other hand. We'd stayed friends since we broke up, and even fooled around occasionally when she asked, though that hadn't happened since June. I think she was really done with me. I was kind of relieved. She was smart, pretty, a great kisser, but I was glad I didn't have to worry about living up to her expectations.

"Don't stress. It's a party! You're supposed to have a good time!"

"I will. But the minute I am *not* having fun, you're going to hear all about it." She pushed her Solo cup full of vodka and cranberry juice into my chest while her other hand intertwined her fingers with mine.

I kissed her hand.

"Save me a dance later?" I asked.

"Will you have time?"

"For you? Of course!"

"Just be safe. Don't overdo it." She pulled her hand away from mine.

"Overdo it?" I asked defensively, taking a step back. Yeah, I liked to have a good time, but I never puked or got belligerent. I knew when to quit.

"If you don't have a ride home, you're welcome to stay over. On the downstairs couch."

"Thanks," I said, jostling the cardboard box. "I better hide these keys." I leaned in and quickly kissed her cheek before I put my captain's hat and sunglasses back on. "I'm not going to forget about that dance," I yelled to her over my shoulder as I waded through the crowd pouring out of the basement and into the garage, high-fiving and welcoming kids I hadn't seen yet.

◌ ◌ ◌

"OH CAPTAIN, MY CAPTAIN! OH CAPTAIN, MY CAPTAIN! OH CAPTAIN, MY CAPTAIN!"

The nice thing about being held upside down above a keg is the feeling of weightlessness. Add a nozzle of frothy Coors Light in your mouth, your head filling up with blood, and your friends cheering you on, and, well, there really is no more freeing way to be.

Most guys would have sputtered and spit up by now, but my record was seven seconds and I was going to beat it.

As soon as everyone chanted "Eight," I jerked my head away. Quincy and Ezra flipped me over and set me down on my feet, raising my arms above me and welcoming the applause. I bowed, which was the worst idea. My head spun and I slipped a little. Derek righted me and held my arm.

"Upsy-daisy," he said. He didn't drink during cross-country or baseball season, but when it was wintertime, I was his designated driver. But even then he'd only have a beer or two.

"Go, Celtics!" I yelled, and the partygoers cheered over the music bumping from a boom box. Derek stayed by my side until he was sure of my footing.

"I think I'm going to head out soon," Derek said.

"What? Why? The party's just getting started," I protested, even though the crowd was definitely thinning out. "I thought you were going to talk to girls?"

"I did. And they left about an hour ago," Derek said.

"But it's so early," I said.

"It's almost one a.m., Maz," Derek said. Really? It didn't feel that late at all. "You need a ride or are you going to stay?"

I couldn't believe he was going to bail.

"When were you thinking of leaving?" I asked, my eyelids suddenly heavy.

"Twenty minutes," Derek said, his voice firm enough to let me know he was going to leave with or without me.

"Okay. Just a minute." I meandered over to where Stacey and two of her friends, Candace and Marisa, were starting to clean, picking up discarded cans and putting them in garbage bags. "How about that dance?" I asked the back of Stacey's head.

She stiffened before she turned around to face me. Her cheeks were red and she was giving me a death stare. "What?"

Suddenly I could smell the vomit. I put my hand over my mouth.

"Don't you dare!"

I swallowed until I knew I was okay.

I reached for the garbage bag in her hand. "I can help." She ripped it away from me.

"I've got it," she said, looking me up and down. "You're soaked." It was mostly sweat, but some of it was beer from the keg. After a second, her expression softened—she looked sad, maybe even pitying. I didn't like it. She didn't know about Sam, but it felt like she did. *There goes sad Maz. Ghost Boy's friend.*

"I'm gonna go with Derek." I straightened up, only wobbling a little. "The keys are under the living room couch. I'll come by tomorrow to help clean up."

"No. Don't," she said, still looking at me like I was a lost cause. "You've done enough. Just . . . take care of yourself, Maz." She walked away, carrying the trash bag with her.

Derek brought me in through the side door, set me on a couch in his room, and put a trash can next to me. "I don't need that!" I said.

He went downstairs to talk to his mom. I tried to listen. Something about "his parents know he's here" and "I thought you said you were going to the movies," but then I lost track.

Derek came into his room and closed the door behind him. He looked at me and shook his head. "Having trouble there?"

My shirt was having a tough time coming over my head. I pulled at it. I heard it rip before I managed to take it off. Derek walked to his bureau drawer, pulled out a T-shirt, and tossed it my way.

"Thanks," I said, but didn't move to put it on. "You think Stacey was mad at me? She was kind of weird tonight."

Derek turned on the lamp by his bed before flipping off the overhead lights.

"The place was pretty wrecked," he said, throwing me a pillow. I almost caught it. "I have a feeling Stacey's not going to cohost a party with you for a while."

"It's just because we broke up," I said, scooping the pillow up off the floor. "If we were still together, she wouldn't have been so uptight."

"Uh-huh," Derek said, taking off his shirt and tossing it in his hamper. "You never said why you two broke up over the summer anyway."

"I dunno. Something about how I didn't open up enough,"

I said, then blew a raspberry with my lips. I was still sitting up but was really looking forward to lying down.

"I could see that," Derek said, getting under the covers.

"What's that supposed to mean?" I asked, brushing a couple curls out of my eyes to get a better look at him.

"Forget it." Derek's fingers were on the lamp cord, but he didn't pull. "Actually I guess I might as well get it off my chest. There's a fifty-fifty chance you won't remember what I say in the morning."

"I'll remember," I said.

"Okay. We've been friends for years now and you're my main guy, especially at Carter." Our prep school was mostly a sea of WASPs where both of us stuck out. Derek was Armenian on his father's side and Jewish on his mother's. Even when Derek and I were part of the "Carter family," there were certain kids who would probably never have us over for a clambake at their summer homes or invite us for a round of golf at the country club. "We talk about everything. Girls, movies, music, school, sports. But sometimes it feels like I tell you everything and you want to keep things pretty surface. You always come over to my house and spend time with my family, but you never invite me over to yours. I've met your family, but you barely let me talk to them. It feels like you don't want anybody to really know much about you."

"Lots of people know me," I said, throwing my hands in the air. "I mean, I'm the Party Captain!"

"You don't have to be a jester for them," Derek said. "There's having a good time, and then there's maybe having a problem."

"Are you saying you think I'm a drunk?" I asked with a laugh. The guys on *Cheers* always made it look fun. But I wasn't like them. Those guys were kind of pathetic.

"I don't know about that," Derek said. "But you've been drinking more and more lately. Stacey's worried about you. I told her you're fine . . . but are you? I mean, you don't look right, Maz."

"Stacey doesn't need to worry about me anymore," I said, realizing it was officially done. "You don't need to worry either. I'm just trying to have a good time!"

"It doesn't look like a good time, man. It looks like punishment." If I wanted a lecture, I would have stayed at home. "That girl, Cori. The one we saw at the mall. You never mentioned her before, but you said she was your best friend. How come you never brought her up?"

"Don't!" I yelled. I saw him flinch. I never lost my cool. "Sorry," I slurred softly. "I don't like revisiting it."

He didn't push. Instead, he pulled on the cord of his lamp.

"Good night, Maz," Derek said in the dark.

10.

MAZ

MY MOM AND I WALKED INTO THE KITCHEN just as Sam set down the receiver. "Can I help you with anything, Mrs. Shahzad?" he asked, the cheer in his voice a little forced.

"That's so sweet of you, Sam. But I think Maziyar should be asking as you are our guest." Sam was rude everywhere except for my house. I couldn't tell if it was out of respect for my family or so I would look like the Goofus to his Gallant. It was probably a combination of both. "Why don't you sit next to Nilou?"

Sam plopped down next to my sister. The corners of her mouth were red from the cranberry juice she was drinking.

"Hey, Lulu. What's happening?" he asked, holding out his hand for a low five. Sam seemed totally fine, like nothing happened at Rob's. His eyes were normal and he wasn't foaming at the mouth. He looked okay. We hadn't told my mom about it.

"Nothing because I can't watch the movie with you." Nilou's lips pushed out in a pout only a seven-year-old could perfect. We had a VHS of *Indiana Jones and the Temple of Doom* to watch after dinner, but after Sam went home in the morning, I wasn't going to be able to watch TV for a while. My mom had also said I had to write Vickie a letter apologizing for what happened and read it to her, even though it wasn't my fault. (I didn't read it aloud, but I passed it to her in class the next week and she seemed happy to get it.)

"That movie is too scary for you, Nilou joon," Mom said.

"It's not scary if Sam watches it!" Nilou insisted. "He's scared of E.T."

"Aren't *you*?" Sam asked. "When E.T. gets sick and all those astronauts come for him? Gives me the chills!" Sam shook in his seat and gritted his teeth, pretending to freeze to death. "*The chills, Lulu!*"

"You're silly," Nilou said.

"And adorable?" Sam asked, wiggling his eyebrows up and down. We had gotten into so much trouble and he didn't seem to give a rip.

"Nooooo!" she squealed.

"Inside voice, Nilou." Mom handed me the plates.

"Ooooh, you're in trouble," Sam fake-whispered.

"I know you are but what am I?" Nilou mumbled back.

"I know *you* are but what am I?" Sam asked in Pee-wee Herman's voice. She and Sam both thought *Pee-wee's Playhouse* was great, but I thought it was kind of creepy and for babies.

"I know *YOU* are but—"

"Stop," I said, cutting their bit short as I set the plates on the table. One time the two of them went on like that for ten whole minutes.

"She started it," Sam said. I shook my head, but I was relieved he was so normal. I rolled silverware up in paper napkins and put them next to everyone's plate. We always set a place for Dad, even though we never knew what time he would get home from the hospital.

Mom brought the lubia polo over to the table. Sam beamed when he saw it. I think he liked Persian food more than I did.

"It's too bad Cori couldn't be with us," Mom said. Before Nilou was born, Cori was the closest thing she had to a daughter. Even after Nilou came along, Cori was always served first at dinner and always got the last Fudgsicle in a box when the three of us would argue over it.

I heard the front door open and shut.

"Daddy's home!" Nilou slid out of her chair and ran to the hall.

My dad came in, carrying Nilou with one arm and his briefcase in his other, grinning from ear to ear.

"Hello, everyone," he said. Dad kissed Nilou on her cheek before he set her down and kissed Mom on both cheeks. Then he took off his coat, loosened his tie, sat at the table, and smiled at Sam.

"Sam! How are things? How's Dave?" Something was up. My dad never asked how Sam's father was. They didn't dislike each other, but they didn't have all that much in common, even back when we were neighbors. When we first moved to the States, we lived in a small apartment in Sam's building. My dad had to redo a lot of training to be certified to practice medicine in America. But when I was nine, he was fully credentialed and the apartment life was traded for a suburban home.

My mom was always the one to ask about Mr. Bennett. She'd pack him leftovers for Sam to take home. Every time, Mr. Bennett would call and thank her and tell her she shouldn't have, but Sam said his dad always looked relieved to find her Tupperware in the fridge.

"He's seeing a woman named Linda. She's lasted a few months, so you know, we'll see," Sam said. He didn't mention Florida. Mr. Bennett had had a lot of girlfriends over the years. They were one of the main reasons Sam spent so much time at our house.

"That's wonderful," Dad said, helping himself to food. I glanced over at Sam. His mouth was open and his brow furrowed like when he was in class and didn't know the answer to a math problem. It wasn't that my dad was a grump, but he wasn't normally this *animated*. Usually when he came home, he was exhausted and didn't talk a lot. He'd nod, smile, say things like "That's nice."

"How are *you*, Dr. S.?" Sam asked.

Dad leaned back in his chair, put down his fork, and stared right at Sam. "Sammy, I am fantastic," Dad said. "I have my beautiful family all together, work is good, the weather is great, and seeing your face fills my heart with joy."

"Daddy is being fun," Nilou said.

"He certainly is," Mom said. "What's going on, Babak?"

"I'll tell you later," he said with a wink. At first Mom looked like she wanted him to tell her now, but then her face brightened. She'd figured out something I clearly didn't understand.

"Are you sure?" she asked, her eyes filling with tears.

"The bank called. We're approved," Dad said.

It took me a minute to put it all together. The whispered conversations. The open house visit they brought Nilou and me to. The Coldwell Banker brochures that Mom looked at sometimes. I remember seeing the cover of one of them that had a giant brick house with flower bushes on either side of a white front door. It was the kind of house you'd find in Brooks's neighborhood.

"We're moving?" I asked.

"Maziyar, we don't know that yet," Mom said, dabbing at her eyes with a napkin. "We'll talk about it later." I knew that meant she didn't want to say anything in front of Sam.

"What about my friends?" I asked.

"You'll still see Sam and Cori if we move," Dad promised. "You can have playdates like always. It'll take a little more planning, but they're welcome to come over anytime." Sam and I looked at each other sadly. We both knew it wasn't true.

❧ ❧ ❧

I woke up to Sam's screaming. I turned on my lamp and found him sitting up in my G.I. Joe sleeping bag, sweat dripping down from his temples, his eyes wide.

"What's wrong?" I hurried out of bed and sat on the floor next to him.

"I, uh, had a nightmare I guess," Sam said, looking around my room and then at me. "I didn't wake up Nilou, did I?"

"I doubt it. She can sleep through anything." Normally Sam slept like a log in my room. He never tossed or turned or even snored; when he was out, he was out. "Must have been some nightmare. What happened?"

Sam kept panting like he'd been running from something.

"This bald old man, like really old and skinny, he was read-ing from this red book. The words he read out loud didn't make sense. It wasn't English or any language I'd heard before. Then he looked right at me. He pointed his bony finger at me and curled it toward him, asking me to come closer, but I didn't. Then he spoke, but his voice was, like, not human. It was too deep and kind of staticky, like he was speaking to me from a radio. He asked me what I wanted. I tried to keep my mind blank, but his lips twisted into this toothy, creepy smile before he disappeared."

Sam closed his eyes, but kept panting. "Then Mom was there."

I froze. Sam almost never talked about his mom after she left. It's hard for me to remember what she was like. Her name was Cynthia, she was young with light brown hair, she'd come over and talk to my mom about *Dynasty* and *Dallas*, and she always wore too much floral perfume that stuck around in the apartment building's elevator. "She looked happy to see me. She spread her arms out. Said she'd been waiting for me, only it wasn't her voice. It sounded like her, but it had that same static, like she was talking through a drive-thru speaker. I wanted to go to her, but I didn't. I'm still so mad at her. Then she stood up, threw her head back, and started to laugh. Her hair fell out, her teeth got sharper and sharper, she breathed fire, and when she turned back to look down at me, her eyes were red just like—"

"Like the eyes on the pinball game?" I asked.

He nodded. I felt cold all over.

"She kept laughing and laughing until her face ripped in half. Her whole body cracked open like an egg until her skin was on the ground like a pile of old clothes. I kept running away from her, but no matter how hard I ran, I could feel the heat from her breath behind me." He opened his eyes and looked so helpless. "Maz? Can you check my back?"

I lifted up his shirt. The skin on his back was covered with tiny bubbling white blisters.

"Holy sh—" I started, but Sam cut me off.

"I think the game . . . I think it did something, Maz," Sam whispered. "I think it wants me."

I tried to call for my parents, but the words wouldn't come out right away. When I finally did, Dad was the first to come in my room.

"What's going on? You two okay?" Dad asked.

"I'm sorry," Sam said.

"Dad," I said, standing up. "You have to look at Sam's back. Something happened."

Dad immediately bent down and lifted up Sam's shirt to inspect him. "Where?" Dad asked, peering at Sam's back.

When I sat down next to him, the blisters were gone. "I— there were burns," I said.

"There were?" Sam asked, sounding more distressed than before.

"I don't see anything," Dad said, the worry in his voice slowly draining.

"Everything all right?" Mom asked from the doorway.

"The boys are fine," Dad said, even though we really weren't.

"I told you not to watch that movie," Mom said.

II.

SAM

I TURNED ON THE COFFEE MACHINE for Dave and then poured myself a bowl of cereal. He and Linda had come in late last night, both of them laughing like they'd had a few drinks. I put my headphones on and pressed PLAY on my Walkman. The mix tape Cori made me almost drowned them out. It was a good tape. Cori put lots of Huey Lewis and the News on there even though she couldn't stand them. Dave's bedroom door opened, and I perked up, until I saw Linda's curly blond hair.

"HI!" I shouted as soon as she walked into the kitchen. She shrieked. "Sorry. Didn't mean to scare you." I'd meant to. It was always fun to mess with Dave's one-night stands, but Linda wasn't a one-night stand anymore. She was "part of our lives" now and the reason we were moving all the way to stupid Florida. "There's coffee if you want some."

She tiptoed to the pot next to the kitchen sink. One of her shoulder pads made its way down her arm. She was cute, even if she looked a bit gray this morning. A little younger than my dad, but not by much.

"You're up early for a Saturday," Linda said, pouring a cup for herself before she sat down across from me. "It must be because it's your favorite day of the year!"

It was sweet that she knew even that much about me, or was at least trying to, but Halloween wasn't the reason I was up early. I hadn't slept at all last night. I didn't want to see the old man again. The nights I could sleep, I'd be having a nice dream about something like throwing balls at a carnival dunk tank target, Tiffany dropping into the water and the crowd cheering me on. But then I'd see that old man sitting in a fancy armchair, his lips moving while he read from that red book. I'd wake myself up before I could hear the gibberish he was saying.

I'd told Maz about some of the nightmares I'd had after that first one, but neither of us could make sense of them. We agreed that the nightmares started when I touched the *Sorcerer* game. We hadn't been to Rob's since. Cori hadn't noticed because she'd been busy with her gal pals. We still hung out after school, even had lunch together, but every other Saturday she went to parties with Vickie and her group. Barf.

"Any plans for tonight?" Linda asked. "Your dad and I can take you to a haunted hayride?" She was trying, but she didn't really know a thing about me.

"I'm going trick-or-treating with Maz and Cori. One last hurrah." I tried not to sound bitter. She took another sip of coffee, then set her I HATE MONDAYS Garfield mug on the table. She opened her mouth to say something, closed it, then opened it again.

"I hope you don't hate me," she said eventually, her voice quiet. "I know it's a lot, asking to move in the middle of sixth grade—"

"Seventh, but who's counting?" That probably wasn't her fault. I wasn't sure if Dave knew which grade I was in. He always asked me if I did my homework, but if I had a question about long division or fractions or something he didn't know right away, he'd tell me to call Maz or Cori. He'd given me the "talk" when I was nine, though. I guess he wanted to make sure I didn't get in the same "situation" he did when he was a teenager, so he was ahead of most parents on that bit of my education.

"Seventh. Right. But with my family's restaurant we're going to have a fresh, new start." Linda's parents were expanding their seafood grill to another location and had asked Linda to run it. Dave was a part of the deal, too, and he seemed to be excited to help in the kitchen. I hate seafood. Barf times twenty. "You'll see. For you, me, your dad, and who knows, maybe one day after your dad and I get married, a new baby brother or sister."

They wanted to have more kids? Who was going to take care of the baby while they were having beers at the bar? Me?

Dave finally came out of his room. He was in his old high school sweatpants and a T-shirt that asked WHERE'S THE BEEF? His hair was tied back in a clean, short ponytail, but his hairline was receding a little.

"Morning, family," Dave said, towering over me. Even though he'd told me I'd have the same growth spurt he did, he promised a lot of things that didn't happen. "Anyone want some eggs?"

"I already ate." The Franken Berry cereal had turned the leftover milk in my bowl pink. "Linda hasn't had any breakfast yet."

"That would be egg-cellent," Linda said. I hadn't seen Dave this happy in a long time, so I didn't roll my eyes or tell her that she was ruining my life. I just put on my best fake grin.

"Hey, tonight's the big night," Dave said as he opened the fridge. "You got a costume?"

"Yup." I had picked our group costume this year.

"Want us to come with you?" Linda asked.

I looked at Dave in panic.

"Nah, he's not a little kid," Dave said, cracking an egg on the edge of the pan with one hand. "You make sure to call me from Cori's when you're done."

❧ ❧ ❧

"You look like you haven't slept in a week," Maz said as we climbed the stairs to Cori's porch. I pulled my mask down over my face. "Another nightmare? Was the old man there again? Your mom?"

"No. They haven't shown up in a couple of days," I said. I pushed the doorbell and heard Potato Chip bark.

Tiffany opened the door, holding a bowl of candy at her hip. She broke out in a fit of guffaws when she saw us.

"You've got to be kidding," Tiffany wheezed.

"Halloween's your time to shine," I said, my voice muffled behind my mask. "You never have to dress up. You're already a monster." This didn't stop her from laughing at us. Maz wasn't any help, he just gaped at her like a chump.

"What are you even supposed to be?" Tiffany asked, holding the bowl in both hands, her laughter dying down. Cori hadn't invited us to carve jack-o'-lanterns with her like we did every year, but there was one next to the door anyway.

"Isn't is obvious?" I asked, holding my gloved hand in the air and pretending to use the Dark Side on her.

"You're . . . RoboCop?" Tiffany asked with a straight face.

"I'm Darth Vader, you airhead," I said. I knew she was teasing, but I wished she'd give it a rest. I was too tired for this.

"Oh yeah, from those movies. What was it called, um . . . *Geek Battles*? *Nerd Combat*?" She bit her lower lip. "I know! *Star Trek*!"

"Is Cori ready?" Maz asked.

"You're happy to walk around with Dork Vader, Maz?" Tiffany asked, looking at him with sympathy. Maz hadn't really put much effort into his costume. He was wearing a black turtleneck and black pants for Luke Skywalker in *Return of the Jedi*. His lightsaber was a flashlight with a green bulb. He didn't even look like Luke, he looked like a singer in a New Wave band with a flashlight. "You don't have to let him boss you around just because he's your father."

"Aren't you supposed to do your job and give us candy?" I said with a sneer. "Since you're home alone on a Saturday night and all."

"You have to say the magic words," Tiffany said.

"Suck—"

"Trick or treat," Maz interrupted.

Tiffany dropped five fun-size candy bars into his pillow-case. Then she picked out only one Tootsie Roll and plopped it in my bag.

"Cori! Maz and Sam are waiting for you," she shouted toward the stairs as she went back into the house. I heard Cori running before I saw her. She rushed to the door.

"What is that?" I asked her, my face heating up. "You're supposed to be Princess Leia!"

We'd been doing group costumes since we were seven, when we dressed as the Three Stooges. That's how Rob came up with our nicknames. Now, this was the last time we got to do this, and she was wearing a long pink dress with a tiara on her head and was holding a bouquet of plastic flowers.

"Happy Halloween to you, too," Cori said quietly. "Vickie invited us all to her house for a party. The girls asked me to be a part of their group costume, we're all supposed to be 'pretty in pink.' They think I'm a prom queen, but I'm actually Carrie before the bucket of blood drops on her. I couldn't say no. You understand, right?"

"No. I don't." I was grateful she couldn't see my eyes welling up behind my mask.

"It's not that big a deal," Cori said.

"It's our last Halloween together!"

Her cheeks got red and her eyes widened, looking like Carrie did when she realized the blood was dripping down her face. Not that I'd seen the movie, I'd just heard Cori talk about it a lot. It sounded too spooky for me. I had enough nightmares as it was.

"How about three more houses and then we head over to Vickie's?" Cori asked us, rubbing her arms to stop shivering. It was a chilly night and Cori wasn't wearing a thick enough coat.

"Sounds good to me," Maz said. We hadn't even made it to Mrs. Bulger's house yet and they wanted to call it quits?

"It's not even seven. And what about the big houses on Chestnut Street?" I said. We always tried to make Halloween last forever.

"There's going to be lots of candy at Vickie's," Cori promised, dropping her fake flowers into her mostly empty sack. "Plus, pizza and a cider-doughnut-eating contest."

"I'm sure there will be bobbing for credit cards, too." I trudged ahead of them.

"Cider doughnuts do sound good," Maz said. The traitor.

"Yup," Cori replied, loud enough for me to hear. "Should be a fun time. Too bad we're out in the cold, scrounging for Bonkers."

I turned around, ripping my mask off my face. "Bonkers are DELICIOUS!" I yelled.

"Whoa, no one is saying they aren't." Maz stepped in between Cori and me.

"You've been spending a lot of time with Icky Vickie. You think she could spare you for one night? Did you tell her I'll be out of your hair in a couple months and you can go over all the time then?"

"I thought it'd be something fun we could all do together," Cori said, wrapping her arms around herself.

"What's wrong with what we're doing now? Trick-or-treating is the best and you two act like I'm dragging you to the dentist."

"Have you noticed that we're the tallest kids out here?" Maz asked me, putting a hand in front of his face like he was embarrassed. "We're only trick-or-treating because we know it's your favorite."

"Oh, well, thank you *so* much for honoring me with your presence." Maybe that's all I was to them now. Someone in the rearview mirror while they went off without me. "I get it. You're going to be neighbors with Brooks Wallington soon, Maz. Who knows, maybe Tiffany will look your way now that you're in a new zip code."

"Shut up!" Cori and Maz shouted in unison.

"Why do you want to go to Vickie's party?" I spat out at Cori. "So Nick the Dick can drool over you all night? You don't even *like* him."

"I don't see what's the big deal with making more friends," Cori said. Even she was getting angry now. I think growing up with Tiffany had taught her to avoid fights at all costs, but right now her teeth were clenched and she gripped her candy sack tight, like she was thinking about throwing it at me.

"Sure, I get it. You both get along fine with the rest of them, but I don't. I'm in the way," I shouted. A group of little witches, ghosts, and Care Bears, along with their parents, stared at us as they shuffled by.

"That's not it!" Cori raised her voice. "When you and Maz leave, who will I have left to hang out with?"

"My parents are just looking at houses," Maz said, but we all knew he was going to move.

"Fine. Go to Vickie's," I said, turning my back on both of them and marching ahead to the next house. I felt a hand on my shoulder. It was Maz and that made me even angrier. I wanted Cori to be the one to come to her senses. She was the one messing the night up and trying to stop me.

"Just a few more houses, Cori," Maz called back to her. I whipped around and got his hand off of me.

But Cori was still mad. "You don't get to be a jerk to us just because you're moving away."

"What's your excuse for being a jerk? You're not moving anywhere," I shouted at her. "You're lying to Vickie and your new friends about your costume. They just think you look pretty." I didn't mean to yell. I was just really tired. Couldn't she tell something was wrong? Was she too busy hanging out with those creeps who called me names to pay attention to the dark circles under my eyes?

"Well, at least they don't act like a toddler having a tantrum," Cori said.

"You're just turning into Tiffany," I said. She scrunched up her nose and tightened her jaw.

"Take it back," Cori hissed.

"Sure thing," I said as I narrowed my eyes. "After we finish Chestnut."

"It's exhausting to take care of you." Boy, she was really on a roll. "When your mom left, I promised you, Maz and I were going to always be there for you and make sure you were okay, but lately it's like you can't stand us—"

I couldn't believe Cori would bring her up.

"Don't you feel sorry for me on the greatest night of the year!" I shouted. I could feel tears wet my cheeks and snot drip down my nose, which was stupid because Darth Vader didn't cry. Only little kids who dressed up like him for Halloween did, and that's all I was to them. "You're ruining everything!"

All the anger in Cori's face disappeared. "Sam, I'm—" She immediately stepped forward, reaching to give me a hug. I recoiled. I didn't want her anywhere near me.

"LEAVE ME ALONE," I screamed. I threw my mask on the ground and ran. I heard them both call out to me, but I ran fast enough to make sure they could never catch up.

❧ ❧ ❧

I sat on the curb across from the diner, wiping my face with the back of my gloved hand. I had been so stupid to think this was going to be a fun night. Cori and Maz kept blaming me for ruining things, when they were the ones being drips all the time.

They don't love you.

There was a voice in my head that wasn't mine. It didn't scare me. It was right. *She* was right.

Nobody loves you.

I would have started crying again, but I didn't feel bad. I felt understood.

Not like the way I love you.

That's not true. You left me.

But I'm back now. You'd like to see me again, wouldn't you?

Yeah.

You can. Join me.

The lights at Rob's turned on. The rest of the stores along the sidewalk were closed, but Rob's would always be open for me. I felt myself stand up.

That's it. You're such a good boy. My sweet boy.

I was inside the store—had it been unlocked? No one else was here. That's okay. I don't need anyone else.

Right. You just need to take care of yourself.

But it's been hard to do that.

Then let me take care of you. Come closer.

She's waiting for me. Inside the game. I'll be happy there. I'll be safe.

Closer.

I don't have to grow up. I can be myself.

Excellent. Now, my sweet Sam, push the button.

Button?

The START *button. Hurry.*

I need a quarter, don't I?

No, you little imbe . . . Please push the button. For Mommy.

Okay.

12

CORI

AS A KID, I always thought interrogation rooms would have a huge spotlight or officers watching from the other side of a mirror, but the one Detective Lambert brought us to was pretty simple. The table was plastic and ready for wear and tear. My dad sat in a swivel chair, and I was in a folding chair.

"Has Sam ever run off before when the three of you have had a fight?" Detective Lambert asked. This was my second time officially speaking with him, and I'd see him maybe three more times after this particular meeting. He'd been nice enough, offering us soda, and he wasn't pushy, but he didn't strike me as someone who thought there was a chance Sam would be found. He looked older than my dad, maybe in his late fifties, and there wasn't much hopefulness in his eyes. He was direct. Said things he felt we needed to know and nothing more.

I shook my head.

"Could you answer verbally for the recording?" Detective Lambert said, pointing to the tape recorder.

"Oh—uh, no. He hasn't," I said.

"Your friend uh . . ." He paused and looked at his notes in front of him. *"Mah-zai-yer,"* he said, mispronouncing the name. "He said in his interview that Sam wasn't sleeping much. Was everything okay for him at home? Did he ever say anything was bothering him or that he felt like running away?"

"He wasn't happy to be moving to Florida," I said. "But he never talked about running away."

"The victim didn't mention he was having any bad dreams?" Detective Lambert asked, picking up his cup of coffee.

"No," I said. I hated that he used the word *victim.* That's all my friend had become. There were search parties of grown-ups out day and night then, looking all over Walnut Mills and the towns surrounding for Sam.

"What about this Rob's Newsstand? That a place you went to often?" Detective Lambert took a long sip of his coffee.

"We hadn't been in a while," I said.

"When was the last time you were there?"

When *was* the last time? I didn't know when we stopped going there, all three of us. School started and I got busy, then I was invited to Vickie's house more often.

"August? I think?"

"Can you remember what happened at the store when you were there?" Detective Lambert asked, clicking a pen and waiting to jot down anything I might say.

Detective Lambert wrote down a few things as I went over all of it again. I kept looking at the tape recorder and wondering who else was going to hear this. Had I said the wrong thing or had I sounded like a freak? He stopped taking notes and looked up at my dad first, then me.

"Your friend, he said the . . ." Detective Lambert flipped through some pages and read aloud what he was looking for. "*Sorcerer* game, it affected Sam in some way. He seemed pretty agitated. Can you corroborate, er—confirm his story?"

I tried to think if I had seen anything. I knew Maz was as upset as I was, but there wasn't any way that dumb game could have hurt Sam.

"Did you see something, pumpkin?" Dad asked. He called me that a lot in those months.

"No," I said. "But Sam did call me later that night at my friend Vickie's. He said he thought like maybe Maz was right. Sam said he felt like someone was with him, but I didn't know what that meant. He hung up after that."

When the interview was finished, Detective Lambert walked us to the front of the precinct. There weren't too many officers, and the ones that were there were taking phone calls at their cubicles. I looked at the bulletin board. Sam's face was on a crisp white flyer with a MISSING CHILD banner above his head. He was tacked next to office memos, a WANTED poster, and so many other flyers of missing people, from all over parts of Massachusetts, ones that had yellowed, their ink faded.

"Kids deal with trauma in different ways," I heard Detective Lambert say to my dad.

"But a pinball machine?" Dad said. "Poor kid is really taking this hard." I thought I heard a hint of relief in his voice. He knew I was "taking this hard," too, but at least I wasn't making up stories.

I looked at the dates on the MISSING photos—the oldest one I saw was from five years ago—and wondered how long a flyer was meant to stay up. Who decided how much time should pass before it was just taken off the board completely?

13.

MAZ

"I KNOW THIS IS DIFFICULT," Dad said from the driver seat. "But you cannot imagine how difficult this is going to be for Mr. Bennett." Mom looked at me and took a deep breath. She was doing her best to keep a brave face, but she had tissues in her purse.

I understand now why Mr. Bennett had agreed to a memorial service for Sam, but at the time, I couldn't believe it was happening. It had only been a few months and he was letting everybody convince him Sam was gone forever.

"We are all going to be very respectful," Dad continued. "Mr. Bennett needs our support." I had a feeling this was the voice he used when he had to tell next of kin a patient didn't make it. Dad didn't talk about work, but there were days when he came home looking worn out. "We're going to ignore the press, walk inside, and give our condolences."

My parents kept their eyes on me. It became too much, so I looked out the window at our old elementary school building.

Sam wouldn't have believed that Principal Burchfield, who was always more than happy to call Sam into her office for disrupting class, had offered the gym as a space for the memorial.

"Maziyar, we all *loved* Sam so much," Mom said in Farsi. "For today, let's focus on how wonderful he was. How grateful we are to have had him in our lives."

They thought he was gone forever, too.

I watched people mill into the gym. Most of them didn't even *know* Sam, never mind like him. Maybe they were trying to be good neighbors, but mostly I think they wanted a front row seat to the evening news. TV vans were parked outside the building and the reporter who knocked on our door (which we didn't answer) was now interviewing our gym teacher, Mr. Drummond. Mr. Drummond used to give Sam a hard time about double dribbling during basketball, so it was weird to see him tearing up.

"I'm not going to say anything to worry anyone," I told them, still not making eye contact. "That's what you're asking. Isn't it?"

When I told Detective Lambert about Sam's nightmares and the game at Rob's, he asked me to step outside so he could talk to my parents. I could see them through the interview room's window, looking more and more worried when he spoke to them. When we got home from the station, Mom explained that Detective Lambert said there were resources if I ever needed to talk to someone. He also told them about how sometimes, when kids experience something painful, they might make up stories to avoid the trauma. Dad said that maybe we should have had a lawyer with us in the room. They didn't want my testimony to go on some permanent record for me. They worried it might hurt *my* future in some way.

They'd had enough of my hoping Sam was alive.

I opened the door and slammed it shut behind me.

❧ ❧ ❧

I pulled at my coat sleeves as I sat and watched the high school chorus sing on stage. A giant poster of Sam's seventh-grade school portrait was on a mounted stand behind them. At least it wasn't the photo they used on his flyers. It felt like everyone was in a dress rehearsal for a funeral, pretending to mourn in case we needed to do it again someday.

Most of the people seated in the foldout chairs were crying, but they didn't even know Sam. The people that did hadn't liked him all that much. Vickie sat up front with her family. She kept looking over her shoulder at Nick, who was directly behind the O'Briens.

When the high school choir started singing "Time After Time," I wanted to laugh. Sam would have cracked up at the fact he was being memorialized with Cyndi Lauper. He would have preferred her theme song from *The Goonies*, but the service wasn't really for him. It was happening so we could cry a bit and then feel less guilty. So that we could get on with the business of forgetting him.

After the song finished, Mrs. Burchfield came up to speak. She used words like *exuberant* and *free-spirited*. What she meant was he was a class clown, disorderly, and someone who would practice drawing Garbage Pail Kids instead of paying attention to a lesson. Apparently, once someone was gone, the polite thing to do was to be less honest about who they really were. Erase the messy stuff to make things simple and clean.

"Now," Mrs. Burchfield announced, "we'd like to welcome Sam's father, David, to say a few words." Mr. Bennett walked up the stairs to the stage that teachers used to remind students about field trip permission slips.

He wore his usual ponytail, but even neater, a navy-blue tie, and a white dress shirt tucked into slacks, his work boots replaced with loafers. He had always been tall and lanky but looked a lot thinner—and older, too.

"I wanted to say thank you to everyone for all of your support," Mr. Bennett mumbled into the microphone, looking at the floor. His nose was pink and his voice sounded scratchy, like he'd been smoking a lot more than usual. I looked at the back of Cori's head. Nick was in the way, but I could see her squirm in her seat.

Mr. Bennett turned his head. He stared at Sam's photograph for a long time. No one said a word. Someone sneezed and no one in that room even uttered a *bless you*.

"I had Sam when I wasn't ready," Mr. Bennett continued, this time looking out into the crowd. He rubbed the stubble on his cheek with a shaky hand. "Cynthia and I, we—we weren't equipped to be all we could be on the parent front. We were barely out of high school, trying to figure out how to raise our beautiful boy. Then when she couldn't stick around, it was just the two of us."

I could see Vickie slump in her seat. When she looked over her shoulder at Becky, her face was scrunched with regret. I guess she hadn't known what Sam's upbringing was like. If she had, would she have been nicer to him? Mr. Bennett put both of his hands on the podium, leaning on it to keep himself up. Sam would have hated seeing his dad that helpless in front of a bunch of strangers.

"I promised myself I was going to do the best I could . . . but I messed up so bad." Mr. Bennett started to cry. His whole body shook. My mom began to cry, too. My dad put his arm around her shoulders. I was glad my parents arranged a playdate for Nilou and she wasn't there to see. All I wanted to do was walk out and scream.

It was Cori who got on stage to hug Mr. Bennett. He held her, and he kept crying until Linda helped him back to his seat. Cori stayed up there. She wasn't tearing up. She looked worn down.

"We'll miss you, Sam," Cori said into the microphone, looking directly at me. "You were one of the best friends I'll ever have." Like everyone else, she was saying goodbye. She wanted me to do the same.

❧ ❧ ❧

My parents and I were first in line to express our condolences to Mr. Bennett as soon as the sham stage show was over. Mr. Bennett sat at a table, his head in his hands, while Linda stood beside him. I hadn't met her before Sam went missing, but Sam never really talked about his dad's girlfriends, unless he pulled a prank on one of them and wanted to brag about it.

"If there's anything we can do, please don't hesitate to ask," Dad said to her. Mom went over to Mr. Bennett and crouched down to embrace him. He sobbed onto her shoulder, his tears leaving a stain on her blazer that grew larger the longer he held on to her.

"Maz," Mr. Bennett said, waving me over after he let go of Mom. "Come here, little buddy." I did as I was told, replacing Mom as though we were tag-team wrestlers and grief was the heel we were fighting. His breath and sweat smelled like alcohol. "I should have been there. I should have taken you kids trick-or-treating. It was my responsibility." He wiped his eyes, but the tears kept coming. "Thanks for always being there for him." Had I been? I should have just gone to stupid Chestnut Street with him on Halloween. I should have tried harder to convince Detective Lambert or anybody that Sam's nightmares weren't just dreams, they were a part of what made him go away. They were a part of that *thing* in Rob's store. I felt like even though he was my best friend, I had somehow wished him away, but I didn't mean to. "He always wanted to go to your house. Always. Loved being a part of a real family, you know?"

"You were a real family," I said. "I should have done more. To stop him. I'm sorry."

Mr. Bennett patted the hair on the back of my neck and then let me go. "You and Cori are always welcome to come see us in Florida," he said.

"You can't go," I whispered.

He looked away. "Too painful to stick around here." I felt dizzy. It was becoming more and more final when it didn't have to be. I backed away from him, unsure of what to do next.

Noisy mourners lined up to grab refreshments, donated by Rob. To his credit, Detective Lambert had investigated Rob's store, then had called my parents to let me know that Rob had cooperated with the cops and they didn't find anything suspect. Rob was shaking hands with Mr. Wallington. I didn't know they knew each other.

I saw Mr. Wallington pass Rob a business card. For a small moment, Rob looked happier than anyone had a right to at a kid's memorial service. Then he remembered where he was, and he put his grief mask back on his face, but I'd seen him take it off.

"You all right?" I heard Tiffany ask behind me. She was in a black dress, her hair up in a bun, and for someone who gave Sam such grief, her mascara was smudged and her eyes had red rims: even Tiffany had been crying.

"No," I said. "You look nice." Did I really say that out loud? I was such an absolute goober. "I was wondering what Rob was talking about with Brooks's dad."

"Probably something to do with business. That's all Mr. Wallington cares about. I haven't seen you at the house in a while."

"I've been busy," I said a little quickly. "How is she?"

"You could go ask her yourself," she said, lifting her chin in Cori's direction. Nick and Vickie stood on either side of her. Cori, sensing my eyes on her, looked at me. She excused herself from her new friends and met me at half court.

"Hey," Cori said. Her hair was down and pulled back with a headband. I was still getting used to seeing her in dresses. "I'm glad you came."

"Yeah, well, that makes one of us," I said. "That was nice, what you did for Mr. Bennett."

"It's the least I could do."

I avoided her eyes, focusing on the scuffmarks on the gym floor. We had seen each other a lot after Sam first disappeared, but only with adults. Whether it was the police or our parents, we'd spent a lot of time trying to talk alone and couldn't. Even at school, people whispered and pointed at us when they didn't think we'd notice; we always had an audience.

"Mr. Bennett said he's leaving," I said, still looking at the floor. "I think it's stupid. He should wait a little."

"Wait for what, Maz?" I don't think she meant to sound cruel.

"It's too soon to give up. Sam wouldn't give up on us." My voice broke a little. I felt Cori's arms around me. I hugged her until I calmed down. I didn't want to cry in front of those phonies.

"There is no *giving up*," she said. "I would love for the police to find him. I would love for him to show up on April Fools' Day and tell us we were ridiculous to worry about him. But it's not going to happen."

I looked past her. Nick and Vickie were watching us. Nick gave me a nod. Vickie took a step forward like she was going to join us, then thought better of it and stayed where she was. Cori followed my gaze.

"What are they doing here?" I asked her.

"Paying their respects," Cori said.

"Why? They never liked him." I knew she was holding back tears when her nose scrunched up. "What?"

"You sounded exactly like Sam just now." I couldn't tell if she was disappointed or touched. "Why didn't you come with us to get pizza on New Year's Eve?" *Us* meant Nick, Vickie, and their whole gang. It didn't mean Sam or me anymore.

"Maybe we could get together, the two of us, and talk. If you want."

"Of course, I want to."

We stood there, not sure really what to say next. That had never happened to us before. We used to be able to talk about anything. Then Mrs. Burchfield came over to us and told Cori that Mr. Bennett was leaving soon and wanted to see her before he left. Cori whispered goodbye to me.

I was on my own. I have been ever since.

14

MAZ

I PARKED MY CAR IN THE LOT where Rob's store, the diner, and all the mom-and-pop shops of my childhood days had been. The diner was closed up for good, and judging by the BIG SALE banners out front, it looked like other stores were on their way out, too. Rob's was empty and had been for six months. A cardboard sign up in his window read THANKS FOR THE MEMORIES! It was six in the morning, early enough that I wouldn't have to worry about bumping into anyone I knew from back then.

I didn't tell my parents I liked to run in our old neighborhood, but once a week, I retraced our old trick-or-treating route, trying again and again to figure out what had happened.

I put my car key in the fanny pack that Derek constantly mocked, stretched my quads, and then set out on my run. There was no one I could talk to about the catatonic squirrel. Even the greatest of friends can handle only so much.

I ran by Cori's house, glancing up at her bedroom window. The lights were out. The only sound, other than my feet pounding against the pavement, came from a few morning songbirds. I imagined the birds choked into silence, lying stiff on the ground with bulging eyes staring at me, and felt myself shiver. I shook my head, willing the image out of my mind, then picked up my pace.

I knew what I had heard the other day. That whistling wasn't a figment of my imagination.

I turned onto my old street, listening to my breathing, taking in the crisp morning air, and letting out the tightness in my chest that came from worry. In, out, in, out, this was what made sense. As long as I focused on my breathing, everything would be okay.

In and out.

There was a figure up ahead, standing on the front lawn of my old house, staring up at my old bedroom window.

In and out.

I squinted. It was still too far away to see.

In and out.

It was a kid. Shrouded in black. I could feel my heart beat in my ears.

In and . . .

The figure turned to me, his black cape dangling in the air behind him. I stopped, twenty feet away from a memory. That's all he was.

"You got tall," the memory said. I closed my eyes, counted to five, then opened them, knowing I would find him gone. But he was still there, only now he stepped toward me. I leaped back. I wanted to speak, but I couldn't. He hadn't aged a day. "Hey, Maz."

"You're not real," I managed, but I could see the wind blowing his cape. I could see him grinning at me like we were seven and he was about to tell me a great prank he wanted to pull on one of our teachers.

"Don't be chickenshit!" Sam said in a comically high-pitched voice, imitating the little girl from *The Monster Squad*.

I got woozy and fell to my knees, staring at the asphalt. I let out a sob I'd been holding in for years.

15.

CORI

"GO, NICK!" I whooped from the bleachers. We were down by six, but the crowd cheered and swelled with school pride. Nick pointed to me from the field. I smiled and waved, for him and also a little for anyone who might be watching.

It was the third quarter of a home game that seemed unbearably long, but then again, they all felt like a waste of time. At least the weather was cooperating. Nick huddled up with his teammates, calling the next play for the Tigers.

"So, what time's the party at your house?" Vickie asked. She stood when I stood, sat when I sat, cheered when I cheered.

"What?" I didn't let my smile falter.

"Your parents are out of town, aren't they?"

"They're going to a funeral. I don't think it'd be great for them to come home and find the house trashed." The only person I had asked to come over was Janet. I wanted her all to myself.

"You're going to hang out with the team after the game, right? Or are you going to hide out again?"

96

"I don't hide out," I said, keeping my gaze focused on the hulking boys crashing into one another.

"That's what I tell Nick. I say you're busy with school and all your *art* projects."

I didn't like the way she said *art*, as though it were a euphemism for something salacious, even though I wished it was. My stomach flipped when I imagined Janet and me alone in the dark room. A whistle blew and not a moment too soon.

"You think I should be at his every beck and call?"

"He's your boyfriend," she said. "I shouldn't have to be the one keeping him posted on your life."

"That's right. He is *my* boyfriend." I turned slightly and gave her an icy stare. She kept looking at the field, but her cheeks flushed scarlet.

I returned my attention to the game. The referees were talking with each other about some penalty while our coach paced the sidelines and yelled his own opinion. A shadow spread across my legs. When I looked up to see who it belonged to, I was surprised to find Maz, blocking the stairs in between the risers.

"Hi, Cori," he said, a little breathless.

"Blast from the past!" Vickie exclaimed. "What are you doing here? Sorry, I mean, hi." Vickie stood up and gave Maz an awkward hug. "How have you been?" I didn't get up. In all these years he'd never come to find me at school. This couldn't be good.

"Hey, Vickie! Long time, no see. I'm okay. You?" He spoke to Vickie but made eye contact with me. I could tell he had been crying. His eyelashes gave him away.

"Fine. Just fine," Vickie answered with a wicked smirk. She looked between us. "Are you here to help Cori out with her *art* projects?"

I almost laughed. She thought I was sneaking around with Maz?

"Uh, no, but I was hoping I could talk to Cori," he said. "Privately."

"Oh. *Priii*-vately."

"Real mature," I told Vickie before turning to Maz. "Look, now isn't a great time."

"Please," he said. His voice was solid but his eyes were huge and bright and he looked like a little kid again. "It's important." It must have been. He wouldn't be here if it weren't.

"Everything okay?" I asked.

"I hope so," he said with a small laugh. "I was hoping you could come with me. I . . . It's a family thing."

I felt a pang of worry in my chest. Memories flooded back of birthday parties, holiday celebrations, water balloon fights. Almost every strong memory I had from childhood involved him and his home.

I stepped over Vickie and asked her to cover for me. The whistle blew and the crowd cheered as we walked down the stairs.

❧ ❧ ❧

"Are your parents okay?" I asked as we reached the parking lot.

"Yes," he said.

I stopped following him. "Then what's the emergency?"

"You'll see," he said, taking steps ahead of me.

Why was his car parked so far away when there were empty spaces everywhere?

"You're freaking me out."

"That's why we stopped hanging out, isn't it?"

I didn't answer. We both knew he was right.

He turned around and stood still, giving me enough room to back away. "There's someone who wants to see you. It's a good thing. I think."

"You think?" I asked.

He beamed at me. "I think it's awesome . . . but I'm in over my head, and I'm not sure what I'm doing. I could use a friend right now."

I could use one, too. I had plenty of people in my life, but none of them knew me as well as Maz once did. Not even Janet.

"Where did you park? Siberia?" I asked as I caught up. He let out a chuckle that was equally nervous and giddy. We finally reached his car. He was parked beside the dumpsters behind the cafeteria, a place kids went to sneak a smoke.

"That's your car?" I asked with a laugh. He'd gotten a black Mustang, almost exactly like the one Brooks used to drive Tiffany around in. "You can't be serious?"

"I know, it's stupid," he said sheepishly. "It's going to be okay."

"What is?" Someone in a red hoodie sat in the front seat. Maz opened the door.

The person turned to us. It was a boy, with pale skin, and—

"You got boobs! Weird!" he said.

The sweatshirt was so big on him, he had to roll the sleeves up to take off his glasses and push the hood off of his shaggy hair. I laughed a little at first, not quite understanding who or what I was seeing. Then the pieces of memory collapsed together onto themselves, exploding with fury.

"I missed you, Cori."

16.

MAZ

I NEEDED CORI TO MAKE SOME KIND OF NOISE, but she was deathly silent.

"Is she okay?" Sam asked.

That's when she started screaming. I put one hand lightly on her shoulder and shushed her, but it wasn't doing much to stop her bloodcurdling wails. Sam put his fingers in his ears. He looked amused, like he'd played the ultimate prank on her.

She fell to the ground, continuing to scream as she scooted away. I crouched down in front of her, trying to get her to look at me, but her eyes were wide and only focused on Sam.

"Cori, I know it's a lot, but you have to calm down or people will notice."

Her screams turned to swears, which I took as a sign that she had heard me.

Sam leaned toward us from the passenger seat and wiggled his eyebrows. "I don't look that bad, do I?" he asked, smirking. He was enjoying this.

"What is happening?" Cori gasped. I gently took her head in my hands and made her look at me, not him.

"It's Sam." She started tearing up. I said it again. "It's Sam. He's our friend." And again. And again. Until eventually, she quieted down.

"He's back?" she whispered in the tiniest voice. I nodded and smiled. Her breathing steadied.

"This isn't exactly the happy reunion I had hoped for," Sam said.

"He's back." She said it so quietly this time, I could barely hear her. "He's the same as when he—"

"I know," I said.

"How is this possible?"

"No idea." I tried to suppress my grin.

"Is he a vampire?" Cori asked.

"Ugh, I wish. That'd be so cool," Sam answered for me. "Also, I'm right here. You can ask me."

"Maybe we should talk in the car?" I suggested. I stood up and offered Cori my hand. She looked at me for a long moment before taking it. I pulled her to her feet. Cori didn't get in the car, so I stood next to her by the open driver-side door. She peered in at Sam, analyzing every inch of him.

"What was the name of your favorite toy?" she asked. I knew that one. It was his Battle Cat action figure from *Masters of the Universe*. "The truth, so I know it's really you."

"Huckleberry Pie," Sam grumbled, blushing.

"What?" I asked.

"From *Strawberry Shortcake*," Cori said in awe.

"I liked the smell, okay?" Sam said defensively. Cori opened the door to the back seat and climbed in.

In the car, Cori and I both stared at Sam, but he gave Cori his undivided attention.

"You jerk," she said, her arms folded across her chest. "Do you know what you put us through?"

"It wasn't my fault," Sam protested, shaking the sleeves of the hoodie back over his hands. "I can't help it if I've been out of the loop for a while."

"Five years!" Cori yelled.

"Yeah! Maz told me!" Sam yelled back.

"Did he also tell you he kept insisting we should keep looking for you and how his family thought he was losing it?" Cori asked. "Or how I cried over you every night for months? How our families watched us like hawks? Our classmates thought we were freaks?"

"No. Maz told me he missed me and that he's glad I'm back," Sam said quietly. "It'd be rad if you could do the same."

Cori studied him and didn't say anything. After a few moments of staring at each other, Sam tucked his upper lip so his gums showed, then flared his nostrils, making the funny face that used to always crack us up. I laughed. She didn't.

"You haven't changed at all," Cori said. "You're so small! Were you always that small?"

"Hey! Watch it." There was some real hurt in Sam's voice.

Then she looked at me. "Why is he back now?"

"We hadn't gotten to that yet," I said, trying to keep the annoyance out of my voice. Couldn't we enjoy this for a minute?

I'd spent so much time trying to push him out of my thoughts. Now I didn't have to.

"Boy, you sure know how to make a guy feel welcome," Sam said.

"Where have you been?" Cori asked, her tone a little softer. "Where did you take off to that night?"

"You mean after you guys decided you were too cool to trick-or-treat?" Cori's shoulders sank, but she didn't look away. "At first, all I wanted to do was get as far away from you two as I could. Then I lost steam, started to walk back home. I saw Rob's was open."

"Rob's was never open that late at night." She was right. He always closed at exactly six.

"Well, the lights were on," Sam said with a sad shrug. "Really, really bright ones that changed colors from yellow to orange to bright blue. I felt like I had to go in."

"What do you mean?" Cori asked.

"I mean, I was being called into the store."

"By Rob?"

Sam shook his head.

"Rob wasn't in there. Nobody was. I heard a voice that I thought was my mom's. I opened the door, went inside, and did what she told me to do," Sam said nonchalantly.

I felt the skin on my forearms prickle. Cori and I shared the briefest of glances, and for a minute our eyes argued over which one of us would ask the next question.

"What . . . what did she want you to do?" Cori said. Her voice was steady, but there were droplets of sweat forming on her upper lip.

"She told me to push START. On the pinball machine," Sam said, then switched to his Pee-wee impression. "Duh!" Cori and I didn't make a sound. Sam rolled his eyes before continuing in his normal tone. "I got sucked into the pinball machine."

I sat there in silence for what felt like a whole minute. Then I actually laughed. A relief that I hadn't ever expected cascaded through my body and left me limp. I leaned against the car door. Cori gawked at me while Sam pushed his lips together and poked them out, looking like a bored duck.

"I-I'm sorry I just—" I started. "I spent all this time thinking something was wrong with me, but there wasn't." Cori looked at me with what I thought was pity, but I didn't need that from her.

She leaned in closer to Sam. "How did it suck you in?"

"I don't know, Cori!" Sam said, exasperated. "There isn't a manual in there! It called out to me, it got really bright so I couldn't see anything, then I was somewhere that wasn't here. You want proof? It's apparently been five years and I'm still twelve."

"Holy shit," Cori whispered.

"Cori swore!" Sam proclaimed, bouncing in his seat, his mouth open in delighted shock.

"We should figure out another place to, um . . . continue this discussion before the game is over," I said. The last thing we needed was everyone seeing Ghost Boy.

"Yeah! Let's head over to Maz's!" Sam said. His excitement made my chest ache.

"I don't think that's a good idea." I trusted my family, but all we needed was Nilou telling one of her friends and the news would be out. We had already dealt with one media circus. I didn't want to think of what might happen to Sam during another one. Would he be studied in some lab by the government, or by a cosmetic company for his antiaging properties? Sent to a facility to live alone?

"You're right," Cori agreed. "We have to hide him until we figure out what to do next."

Sam turned my radio on. Music blasted from the speakers. I switched it off, hoping no one heard us.

"Thanks for the warm welcome, guys," Sam said. "Really, I'm touched."

I ruffled his hair and pulled him in for a hug. "Sorry. We're so sorry." When I let go, I realized Cori hadn't touched him once.

"Sam, was there anyone else in the machine with you?" Cori asked.

Sam perked up in his seat. "Yeah! How'd you know?"

17.

CORI

WE DIDN'T ALWAYS HAVE THE TELEVISION ON during family dinner, but that night Tiffany was paying us an unexpected visit for the long weekend and she hadn't been in much of a talking mood, so my parents left the local news on. Potato Chip even noticed the tension, quietly staying by my feet and not whining for scraps like he usually would.

"The chicken's great, honey," Dad said, some breadcrumbs sticking to the bottom of his mustache.

"Thank you." Mom cut her asparagus, while shooting concerned glances at Tiffany, who was smushing her mashed potatoes with a fork. "Cori, any plans this weekend?"

"Not really." I think I ended up spending that weekend at the mall with Vickie and Becky.

The phone rang. Tiffany sat up, breaking out of her gloom.

"Tell him I'm not here," she said.

"This again?" Dad grumbled. I didn't say anything, but I sort of agreed. I could barely keep track of when Tiffany and

Brooks were together or broken up. Mom just nodded and picked up the phone.

"Hello? Oh, hello, Brooks. How are you? How are you liking college?"

Tiffany stabbed her fork into her untouched piece of chicken.

"Tiffany can't come to the phone right now, Brooks," Mom apologized.

My sister rolled her eyes. "I told her to say I wasn't here," she hissed.

"You want me to make sure he stops calling?" Dad asked.

"You'd have to ask her that. I don't know about anyone named Steve," Mom was saying to Brooks.

Tiffany slammed her hands on the table and rushed over. Potato Chip barked, ready to go into battle if she needed him. Mom handed the phone to her with a disappointed shrug and then came back to the table. The three of us continued to eat our dinner as quietly as possible while Potato Chip continued to bark and Tiffany berated Brooks for spending time with a girl that was not her at a frat party.

"I don't like it," Mom said, cutting up asparagus instead of eating it. "She's too attached to that boy."

"She could do worse," Dad said between bites of chicken.

"What do you mean it's Greek Week and you have to be on your A game?" Tiffany yelled. "You'd rather get spanked by some senior guys than spend time with your girlfriend?"

"Spanking?" Mom asked, alarmed. Her eyes flew to the phone.

"Honey, don't get involved. It only makes it worse," Dad said.

My parents continued to analyze Tiffany's side of the conversation while I tried to zone out until I could be excused. I patted Potato Chip's head to calm him down and turned toward the television. I saw a photo of a white, heavy-set man with text underneath it reading MISSING: BILL DOHERTY, AGE 47. His face was familiar, but it took me a minute to place him as the same man who used to scratch lottery tickets at Rob's.

I got up and walked toward the television. I turned the dial to raise the volume. The newswoman's voiceover introduced Susan Doherty, Bill's elderly mother. Mrs. Doherty had orange hair with white roots. She was tiny and frail. So different from her burly son.

"I know he's a grown man, but he's never been gone from home this long before." Mrs. Doherty's thick Boston accent colored every word she said into the reporter's microphone. "The police said I had to wait forty-eight hours to call, but it's been more than that and they think I'm being silly. Just because your child is an adult doesn't mean they're not your baby anymore."

I wanted to call Maz and ask him if he knew about this, but we hadn't spoken since he started at his new school. I wanted him to call first to tell me he was sorry, that he came to his senses, that we could grab a bite to eat sometime to catch up. He never did.

"*No!*" Tiffany bellowed. "*I* said we should see other people. *You* said you couldn't live without me and that I'm always on your mind blah, blah, blah."

Obviously some things were better off staying in the past.

18.

CORI

IT WAS STRANGE ENOUGH TO RIDE AROUND with Maz in a car that he bought to impress Tiffany, or girls like her, but it was surreal to listen to Maz explain the plot of *The Karate Kid Part III* to our long-lost friend.

"Daniel almost joined Cobra Kai?" Sam raised his eyebrows in disbelief.

"Sort of," Maz said as we pulled into my driveway. "I thought it'd be cool, but they should have stopped at Part Two." Maz put the car in park and looked back at me with a small grin on his face. Why wasn't he at all worried about what was going on? He acted like this was some great do-over, wrongs had been magically righted, and now we were all going to have some happily ever after, but none of this made sense. A rubber band of dread in my stomach felt like it was about to snap.

"Let's go," I said as I got out of the ghost of Brooks's car. I could hear Potato Chip scratching at the front door waiting for me to unlock it. I held him back so Maz and Sam could enter.

"Potato Chip!" Sam exclaimed, bending down to pet my dog. "How've you been, buddy?" PC sniffed Sam's hand, recognized the scent, and leaned into him, barking excitedly and wagging his tail. Sam scooped my dog up and stood beside me, and his arm brushed against my hip. Without thinking, I edged away from him. I saw Maz notice, but he didn't say anything. Sam looked and acted the same . . . but there was too much about him that I couldn't explain.

"Can I, um, get you guys anything?" I asked. "Water or juice or something?" It sounded so stupid as it came out of my mouth, but it was better than *What the hell is happening? What are we going to do? Why on Earth did I invite you into my house because you might be a vampire even though you said you aren't*, etc.

"What a hostess," Sam said to Potato Chip before looking up at me. "I'm good, but Maz needs to rehydrate after all that running and crying."

I turned to Maz, who shrugged and laughed. Sam followed me into the kitchen and sat at the table while I got Maz a glass of water.

"Place hasn't changed a bit," he said with satisfaction. "You two sure have, though. Maz, you got so tall and you've got a jawline like a G.I. Joe action figure!"

Maz rubbed his hand through his hair, the curls springing up after he let them go.

"I'm a real American hero," Maz said with a mixture of pride and foolishness as he took the glass of water from me.

"Now all you need is muscles," Sam said.

"Dude! I have muscles," Maz said, insulted, taking off his letterman jacket and flexing his hardly-there biceps. "See?" Sam squinted, then shook his head. Maz was sinewy and in shape, but he was skinny in a way that made me wonder if he was eating enough. "Oh yeah? Check out my calves."

"Sam, we have some things to discuss," I said, interrupting Maz's . . . whatever that was, suddenly wary of how familiar Sam was with the inside of my house.

"That I was in a pinball machine for years?" Sam asked. "Gee, Cori, can't we catch up a little first? Shoot the breeze? Bake some Shrinky Dinks in the oven?"

He was still such a smartass.

"What's it like in there?" Maz asked. Apparently he believed Sam's story. I couldn't deny that Sam was still twelve, which made no sense, but the truth had to be more realistic than being trapped in a pinball machine. Sam was hiding something from us, but I didn't know how to even imagine what it was.

"It definitely didn't feel like years," Sam began. "More like a couple of minutes or maybe an hour. Time doesn't exist there like it does here. But it's not bad. It's warm, feels good. Kind of like when I had my tonsils taken out, and the doctor told me to count down from ten to one, but I couldn't remember falling asleep."

Maz took a sip of water. He used both hands to lift the glass, but it still shook a bit. At least this was freaking him out, too.

"Sometimes it feels a little crowded, you know, when you can tune into everyone else in there." Sam spoke about it casually as though he were talking about what chores he did.

"Everyone else?" Maz asked.

"What's wrong with Potato Chip's eyes?" Sam held my dog up, ignoring the question. "They're kind of cloudy."

"The vet told us that sometimes happens to older dogs," I said. "He's going blind."

"Oh." Sam looked at Potato Chip a little more closely. He kissed the top of PC's head before plopping him in his lap.

"Sam, about the others in the machine," I started.

"I can't believe it's been five years," Sam said, his green eyes clear and blazing. "Maz, you can drive now! That's awesome! Did you go to Canobie Lake Park like we said we would?" Sam had always wanted all of us to go up to the New Hampshire amusement park once one of us got our driver's license.

"I didn't. Did you?" Maz asked me. I nodded. Nick had taken me when school let out for the summer, and it was a fun day. He was fine company on the Yankee Cannonball coaster, but I wished he were someone else when he held my hand on the Ferris wheel. Sam looked back and forth between us, his face loosening, losing some of its enthusiasm.

"Why didn't you go with her, Maz?" he asked.

Maz and I looked at each other before either of us said anything. I imagine this is the way parents look at each other when they have to tell their kid that they're getting a divorce.

I was silently grateful when Maz took the lead.

"Some things changed when you were gone," Maz said.

Sam studied my face for a long time and I must have given something away.

"YOU GUYS AREN'T FRIENDS ANYMORE?" he shrieked.

"We're friendly," Maz said to calm Sam down. "I mean, we're at different schools and have busy schedules. Right, Cori?"

"Time changes people, Sam," I said. Unlike Maz, I wasn't

going to sugarcoat things. "Now I have something to show you both. Would you follow me, please?"

Sam blinked at me in surprise, then spoke to Potato Chip again. "I know, they're both so *serious*." Sam mock-frowned. PC barked. Sam jumped up. I flinched. "Lead the way," he said.

Sam and Maz followed me out of the kitchen and through the living room, but when I reached the bottom of the stairs, I was by myself. I turned around to find the boys looking at a framed photograph on the living room wall.

"Coming?" I asked.

They were looking at Brooks and Tiffany's wedding photo. My sister got married at the Wallingtons' summer estate, and the Wallingtons had about ten guests for every single person who attended from our side of the family. Tiffany said that their special day was filled with so many of her father-in-law's business associates that it could have been a tax write-off, which caused yet another fight between her and Brooks. "She really did it." Maz sounded the same way he had when we watched the *Challenger* explode on TV at school and he asked Mr. Drummond if there was a possibility that some of the astronauts survived.

Sam put his hand on Maz's back. "I give them a couple of years," he said before looking up at me. "No offense."

I didn't respond and kept walking to my room. I bent down and pulled a giant box from under my bed. It held all my special issues of *Fangoria*, childhood souvenirs, and my research binder. I pulled it out and put it on my dresser. The boys stood on either side of me.

"Sam, you mentioned there were others with you while you were, um—" I flipped to the two articles about Bill Doherty I had saved and pointed to his photo. "Is this man *with* you?"

"Hey, yeah, there's Bill," Sam said. "I mean, we don't talk much or anything, but we can sense each other in there. Like we're all sharing the same dream, I guess."

"That's the guy who used to get lottery tickets from Rob," Maz said. I flipped through pages of articles and flyers featuring missing people. Sam didn't recognize any until an article from 1988 about Rosie Tomlinson, a fifty-two-year-old mail carrier, single with no children.

"They couldn't have found a better picture of Rosie?" Sam asked. "Yikes, she wouldn't like that one bit." After that, Sam recognized three more people: Alejandro Diaz, a thirty-three-year-old plumber who went missing in 1990; Sally Hughes, a forty-seven-year-old bus driver in '91; and Bobby Clemson, a twenty-one-year-old college dropout in '92. Sam identified all of them.

"I don't get it," Maz said. "You've been collecting this information the entire time and you didn't tell me?"

"What would have happened if I called you, Maz?" I asked him. "We'd have broken out a Ouija board and had some kind of séance?"

"I don't know but—well, maybe that would have worked," Maz mumbled.

"Highly doubtful," I said. "But I'm . . . I apologize for not believing you."

I could see Maz's shoulders relax and his jaw unclench. I felt guilty. He'd held on to that secret by himself for so long.

"Sam," I said. "Did the others leave the machine with you?"

"Nope! It's just me."

"How come?" If what he was saying about the machine was true, why was he the only one to break free?

"Just lucky I guess," Sam said, with a shrug that looked a little forced. "Do you think you could take me to my dad's place, so I can let him know I'm okay?"

I felt my walls dissolve. Maz cleared his throat to speak, but he looked at the floor, unable to even make eye contact with either of us. I was going to have to tell Sam.

"Sam, your dad . . . It was very difficult for him when you, um, when you weren't here," I began. Sam's eyes grew to the size of grapefruits.

"He's dead?" he asked.

"No!" I said quickly. "Sorry, no, he's not dead."

Sam took a deep breath.

"He and Linda went to Florida."

"Oh," Sam said, suddenly interested in my dresser. "How long after?"

I was about to lie and say a few years, but before I could, he cut me off. "Never mind, um, I don't know why I asked that." He blinked a few times and chewed at his lower lip. "May I use your bathroom?"

"Of course," I said, and he rushed out of the room. I turned to Maz, whose eyes were still fixed on the carpet.

"Thank you," he said. "I couldn't say it."

I didn't like being the one to give bad news, but sometimes you had to. It was a part of growing up. Wasn't it?

"What are we going to do about him?" I whispered. "My

parents come home Tuesday, and I am pretty sure they'll call the police."

"We'll figure it out," Maz promised. "He's back! Aren't you happy about that?"

"I don't know," I confessed.

"You're something else," Maz said, shaking his head. "Sam is alive and well."

"We don't know that he's well, Maz."

"If we can find the machine, we can figure out a way to get all those other people out. Think about all the families we'd help, reuniting them with their loved ones."

"You really believe him, don't you?"

"Why are you so quick to dismiss what you can see with your own eyes?"

"Why are you so quick to trust everything he tells us?" I snapped.

"He's my best friend," Maz whispered.

"He *was* your best friend. We don't know what he actually is now." Sam might not have been a vampire, but people didn't just come back from . . . wherever he was.

"He's the same as he always was," Maz said softly, scratching the back of his neck. But this time he sounded like he was trying to convince himself instead of me. I didn't want to fight about why or how Sam was here, but we needed to come up with some sort of plan for how to help him. We couldn't do that without more information.

"I don't believe all of his story, but we should try to find the pinball machine and learn more about where it came from."

"*If* we can find it," Maz said.

The doorbell rang.

"You didn't say you were expecting someone," Maz said, an edge of worry in his voice.

"I'm not . . ." I shook my head, but then I remembered the one person I had wanted to come over this weekend. I heard Sam open the door.

"Hi!" he said. "Your hair is so cool!"

19

MAZ

CORI AND I ALMOST TRIPPED DOWN THE STAIRS. The girl from the mall stood in the front door smiling at Sam, who beamed right back.

"Janet," Cori said, breathless.

"Hi," Janet answered. But when she saw me, her smile vanished. "Did I come at a bad time? You said to come over but maybe I'm early—"

"No, no, I was just . . ." Cori paused. "Hi. You—everything okay?"

"Yes?" Janet asked. "Are *you* okay?"

"I think so." Cori snuck a glance at Sam, who was still smiling. We all stood there staring at one another until the silence became uncomfortable.

"Hi. I'm Maz." I waved a little, trying to seem normal. "We met the other day."

"Yeah. I remember," she said, her voice hard. I didn't know what Cori had said about me, but it must have been terrible.

"I'm S—"

"Come in! Please!" Cori interrupted Sam, pulling Janet's bag off her shoulder and blocking him from her. Cori looked at me with wide eyes, silently demanding that I come up with a cover story as she led Janet into the living room. "Can I get you anything? Have you eaten?"

"I'm all set," Janet said. "Did I interrupt something?"

"No, not at all." Cori stalled for time, dropping on the couch and patting the cushion next to her. Janet sat beside her. "Maz surprised me with a visit."

"Right. Yeah," I explained. "It was so great seeing Cori the other day that I thought I'd come over." Sam watched everything but, thankfully, stayed silent next to me.

"Have we met before?" Janet asked Sam. Cori shot me a rattled look.

"Nope! First time!" Sam answered honestly.

"He's my little brother," I lied. Janet's expression didn't change, but Cori glared at me. "You know, like Big Brothers Big Sisters program."

"Oh. Cool." Janet gave me a real smile.

"I'm learning a lot from this guy." The sarcasm in Sam's voice was obvious. "Like how to fart on command and why girls aren't as smart as boys."

Whatever smile Janet had for me was replaced with a scowl.

"He's kidding! I didn't teach him that," I said. "We were actually going to head out for a while. I promised this little guy I'd get him some new clothes if he got his grades up."

"Watch it with the *little guy* stuff," Sam snapped. We'd been taller than him before, but he must have hated the way we towered over him now.

"Do you think that's a good idea?" Cori asked.

"I think we'll be okay at the Galleria mall." It wasn't the one closest to here. Besides, almost everyone who would remember Sam was still at the football game. "Maybe we can catch up later?"

"Okay! Let me walk you out." Cori sprang up off the couch and rushed us to the door.

"Bye, Maz," I heard Janet say. "Bye . . . I'm sorry, I didn't catch your name."

Sam turned around and sipped an imaginary drink. "Bond. James Bond," he said in his best Sean Connery impression.

"His name's Peter," Cori blurted out, opening the door.

"Peter?" Sam whispered to her. "You going to tell her my last name is Pan, too?"

"You can come up with a last name in the car," Cori whispered back. "Keep a low profile, and I'll see you both at seven."

"Will she be here?" I asked quietly.

"I hope so!" Sam said. "She seems radical."

"I don't know. Just—make sure you're inconspicuous," Cori whispered. "And nobody says *radical* anymore."

❧ ❧ ❧

Sam strutted out of the dressing room in a pair of blue jeans and a sweatshirt with Bart Simpson on the front, the speech bubble above him reading DON'T HAVE A COW, MAN.

"How do I look?" he asked, turning around slowly, his arms extended out on either side. I put my hands up like I was holding up a camera, closed one eye, and pretended to take his picture.

"You look *mah*-velous, darling," I said, doing my best Billy-Crystal-impersonating-Fernando-Lamas on *Saturday Night Live*. Sam posed a little more before he'd had enough and looked down at his sweatshirt.

"Who is this guy anyway?" Sam asked.

"He is right up your alley," I said, picking up the rest of Sam's haul from the chair next to mine: pajamas, underwear, socks, two T-shirts, a sweater, another pair of jeans, and a Red Sox cap. As soon as I put the cap on Sam's head, you couldn't tell him apart from any other kid at the bustling mall. "We'll save formal wear for another day."

I placed the items on the counter and the woman behind the register began to scan them.

"The gentleman will be wearing these out," I said, handing her the tags for the sweatshirt, jeans, and hat.

"My son just loves Bart, but I don't know," the lady with the nametag SUE said. "I sometimes wonder if he's a bad influence."

"Kids will be kids," I said, pulling my Visa out of my fanny pack and handing it to her.

"You've got a credit card?" Sam asked me. "No way! Can we buy a dirt bike?"

"My parents gave it to me for emergencies," I said as Sue raised a that-must-be-nice eyebrow. Some of those emergencies included gas, the occasional CD, movie tickets when I used to take Stacey out, pizzas for the team. So long as the purchases weren't enormous or I could justify them, it wasn't a big deal. "This is a fashion emergency." I signed for the haul while Sue bagged Sam's new wardrobe.

❧ ❧ ❧

"Did America win?" Sam asked. We sat at a table in the corner of the food court near the bathrooms, as far away as possible from other diners, our Burger King meals spread before us.

"I don't know that anybody won the Cold War," I said after swallowing a bite of my Whopper. "I suppose when the Berlin Wall fell, people were pretty happy about it. The Soviet Union isn't so much of a union these days."

"We're not at war anymore?"

"Well, we had another war. The Gulf War, under President Bush, but that's over. It didn't last too long."

"What about the war with Iran and Iraq?" It was sweet of him to ask. Nobody else really did, but my family had spent most of the decade checking in with relatives and friends trying to make sure everyone was safe.

"That ended in '88."

"So Bush is president now?"

"Yeah, but he's running against a guy named Clinton who played the saxophone on the *Arsenio Hall Show*. He admitted he smoked pot once. But he didn't inhale so I guess it doesn't count.

"There's no cure for AIDS and people are still assholes about thinking it's a gay disease, but I think there's more awareness about how it spreads. You remember that kid Ryan White? They wouldn't let him go to school in Indiana because he got HIV from a blood transfusion?"

"Yeah."

"I think he did a lot to change people's minds. When he passed away, there were laws signed to help people with AIDS."

"He died?" Sam's voice cracked, and his face crumpled.

"Yeah. His funeral was on TV. Elton John and Michael Jackson were there. I felt so bad for his mom."

"How old was he?"

"Eighteen." Sam didn't ask any more questions for a few minutes, so I scarfed down some fries. "You're not hungry?" He hadn't touched his Whopper Jr., onion rings, or even his soda.

"No, I'm pretty full," Sam said, sliding the toy that came with his Kids Meal across the table.

"When did you eat?" I asked.

"A while ago," Sam said, pondering his next question. "There are three *Back to the Future*s?" We had to cover all the important matters of record after all.

"Yup. Six *Police Academies*, five *Rocky*s, three *Rambo*s, two *Ghostbusters*, and a partridge in a pear tree."

"Wow. Sly was busy," Sam said. "Did the Patriots win the Super Bowl or the Sox win the World Series?"

I sucked my teeth, winced, and shook my head. He hadn't been gone *that* long.

"What about the Celtics?"

"Not since '86," I said. The three of us had watched a lot of that championship at my house.

"Bruins?" We both laughed at that. Sam and I never cared

about hockey. "He really moved to Florida, huh?" His voice dropped to just above a whisper when he asked.

"He was a real mess, Sam. He thought you were dead. A lot of people did."

"You didn't," Sam said. "Thanks, Maz." Sam held up his hand for a high five. I slapped it, hard, and we both grunted "Buds" at the same time, like we used to. I took one of Sam's untouched onion rings and dipped it in honey mustard. He didn't protest. "What's new in video games?" he asked, nodding his chin in the direction of the arcade.

"I've got a Sega Genesis at home and that's pretty fun. You'll like *Sonic the Hedgehog*. I don't really go for arcade games though."

"How come?"

I gave him a you've-got-to-be-kidding-me look.

"Oh. Right. But I mean, what are the odds that'd happen again? Come on, let's play."

We tried out *Street Fighter 2* and *WWF Wrestlefest*, but his favorite game was the giant six-player *X-Men*. We'd been at it for a while, with me as Cyclops and Sam as Colossus. There was a little girl playing as Storm, and the three of us were working well together. Sam yelled every time he used his power up, wiping all the bad guys out with an explosion of energy. We got to the end without having to feed it more quarters.

"We are on a roll!" Sam exclaimed over the sound effects. "Blow that sucker up!" The little girl and I laughed, then Sam did, too. I hadn't laughed like that in five years. Now that I'd found it again, I never wanted to let the feeling go.

Sam kept feverishly pushing the two buttons over again, occasionally jumping, but mostly landing a punch-kick combination as fast as he could.

"You guys almost done?" a voice cut in.

I glanced over my shoulder. Five boys waited for us to leave. They looked like they were maybe fourteen. The one in front with the MEGADETH T-shirt was beefier than the rest.

"You can join us," I offered.

"We wanna play as a group," said Megadeth kid.

"We're going to be a while," Sam yelled, keeping his focus entirely on the game. Megadeth and two of his friends joined us as Wolverine, Nightcrawler, and Dazzler.

"Aw, man," one of them said. "I'm the dumb girl character. All she does is shoot fireworks out of her hands."

For the next round, we all beat up dinosaur people with pterodactyl heads in relative harmony.

"Cyclops, why are you slacking, man?" Megadeth asked with a laugh. "Pull your weight." I blushed a little, but these kids weren't going to bully me off a stupid arcade game. Eventually Storm died. The girl playing her reached for a quarter to continue, but Megadeth swiped it.

"Hey!" she said. Megadeth held it out of her reach until the countdown hit zero. Ending her run.

"Give it back to her," Sam said, his eyes still fixed on the game. Megadeth did. The girl took the quarter but left to play a different game. One of the boys joined in her place.

"One down, two to go," Megadeth said.

"Cut it out, Mark," one of the others said.

"Why don't you go play Whac-a-Mole or something, kid?" he said to Sam.

These kids had probably been in fourth grade when Sam disappeared. They weren't going to recognize him, but we were supposed to keep a low profile. Causing a scene in a mall arcade over an *X-Men* game was not in our best interest.

"Let's go," I said, stepping back from my joystick mid-fight, Cyclops's image flickering a few times before he finally went down. The last of the other boys took my place, but Sam continued to play. I watched their backs. The glow from the game intensified, the bright colors getting whiter, the boys' silhouettes more pronounced. Sam, the shortest of the group, turned his head slightly toward Megadeth.

Megadeth coughed a little, then cleared his throat. The *X-Men* game's music began to play faster and the graphics became more pixelated, blipping and malfunctioning. One of the boys knocked the side of the game with his fist. It started to play even faster. Megadeth started coughing a lot more. His eyes bulged and his face turned cherry red. Then everything went completely dark. The only light came from the dim blue lamps above us and the doorway to the rest of the mall. All the games in the arcade shut off, screens blank, the only sounds the shouts and complaints of frustrated customers and the hacking, gasping, gurgling coughs of the kid who'd told Sam to leave.

"What's wrong with Mark?" one of the boys asked. I heard Mark wheeze before I saw his shadowy body fall to the ground and his friends rush over to him. "Somebody help! Call nine-one-one!"

The games all turned on in a blaze of electronic glory, each one playing at an unearthly volume. People covered their ears with their hands. *Street Fighter* chanted, "HADOUKEN! HADOUKEN! HADOUKEN!" The Whac-a-Moles hopped up and down frantically, the moles' plastic casing nearly falling off the springs. The kids huddled around Megadeth, who lay on the floor. I could see them shouting for help, but their voices were drowned out by the beeps, buzzes, and theme songs.

Sam kept his back to me, his head still turned in the direction of the kid on the ground.

"He's not breathing!" someone screamed over the noise.

"Sam!" I yelled.

My friend turned around to face me, his green eyes shining underneath his hood and a curl of a smirk on his lips. The games returned to normal. The lights mellowed, and the customers stopped screaming. Megadeth started breathing and, after a few seconds, sat up. His friends helped him to his feet.

"We can go now," Sam said, picking up his shopping bags and strolling past me like nothing had happened. I looked back at Megadeth. He shrugged, trying to play it off, but his eyes were full of fear. He reminded me of the squirrel. I felt my blood turn cold, the ice in my veins painfully familiar.

Cori's voice played in my head. *We don't know what he actually is now.*

He was Sam. He was my best friend.

But something was wrong with him.

20.

CORI

JANET HAD SPENT THE PAST FEW MINUTES sitting cross-legged on my bed reading an issue of *Sassy* magazine. I looked out the window, checking for Maz and Sam. It was still light out, but they had been gone for almost three hours.

"That's your sixth time," she said.

"What?" I tried to will Maz's car down the street.

"Checking the window."

I stepped back.

"And that's maybe your twelfth time pacing back and forth."

I stopped walking. "Sorry," I said.

"Why are you so on edge?" Janet put the magazine down on the comforter, giving me her full attention. "Whatever it is, you can tell me."

I wasn't so sure. I still couldn't explain what had happened today to myself. How would I even begin to explain it to her?

"It's a lot," I said, running my fingers through my hair.

"I know," she said.

129

"You do?"

Janet continued to stare at me, her eyes soft and sympathetic. Had she recognized the Ghost Boy? How was she so chill about it? She was so much braver than I was.

I sat down next to her, relieved I could talk to someone I trusted about . . . everything. Maz was too giddy. I needed someone who could be objective.

"I don't know where to start," I said. Janet took my hand. Without thinking about it, I intertwined my fingers with hers.

"Tell it to me like you would in our cabin," Janet urged. I pictured us rehashing plots from our favorite horror movies and books or improvising stories, making sure we didn't make them too frightening as Cabin 4 giggled, gasped, and eventually, fell asleep. The memory was enough to calm me down.

"I don't know how I thought I could keep it a secret from you," I began, trying to find the right words. "But I didn't want to risk you freaking out or having other people find out."

"You don't have to tell anyone until you're ready," Janet said. "But I want you to know, you're not the only one who feels that way."

"I'm not?" I asked, confused. Janet shook her head. "Thank you. It was hard thinking of having to do this alone. Well, and with Maz, but he's in la-la land right now."

"You told Maz?" Janet asked, her voice louder and sharper. She pulled her hand from mine.

"Well, I didn't tell him. He found out for himself."

"Oh," she said, her cheeks turning a shade of pink that

almost matched the color of the tips of her hair. "He knows about us?"

"What?"

"That we like each other."

I was too stunned to say anything. I was waiting for my body to evaporate and become nothing but dust floating in the air. Her eyes were wide, regret flooding her face. "You weren't talking about *that* were you?" She slid off my bed and stood up, collecting her things. "I should go."

"What? No! Janet, I do—"

"Forget I said anything! I don't know what I was thinking." She hurried from my room. Potato Chip barked as I chased her down the stairs.

"I'm sorry I didn't know—" I said, but she ran out the front door and got in her car, leaving me to watch her drive away. I felt light-headed. She liked me, too. How was it possible to be so sorry and so excited at the same time?

She liked me, too.

21.

MAZ

"HOW LONG DO I HAVE TO WAIT?" Sam was perched on a stool in Cori's bathroom with a clear shower cap on and a towel draped over his new clothes so the bleach wouldn't ruin them.

"Awhile," Cori said, peeling her gloves off and then washing her hands.

"I'm going to look so bitchin'! Right, Maz?"

I nodded from my place in the doorway, trying to force my own enthusiasm. I hadn't told Cori about the arcade. I wanted to wait until we were alone. It wasn't that I was afraid of Sam, but I was afraid about the unpredictability of whatever had happened to him.

"How come Janet didn't stick around?" Sam asked.

"We had a miscommunication." Cori concentrated on the towel she was using to dry her hands.

"What's she like?" he continued.

"She's really great." Cori's voice was sweeter than I'd ever heard it before, like every word was dripping in maple syrup. "She's an amazing photographer. She's into horror like I am, and she has the best taste in music." She caught my eye in the mirror, and her walls came back up. "We talk about a lot of the stuff I used to talk about with you guys. I don't do that with Vickie or Nick."

"Icky Vickie Greenfield?" Sam asked. "You're still hanging out with her? She's the worst!"

I didn't know what Vickie was like as a person now, but she hadn't looked the least bit icky at the game.

"She's not like that anymore," Cori said, turning to look at Sam. "She's been a good friend to me. Most of the time. We can't all be perfect like you, Sam."

"I guess that's true," Sam agreed, missing her sarcasm. "I can't believe you hang out with Nick the Dick though. He's not your boyfriend, is he?"

"He is, actually," Cori said. She didn't sound proud or happy about it. She sounded tired.

"What?" Sam shouted. "He's so boring! All he had going for him was being tall! What do you guys even talk about? Or, gross—do you just want him for his body or something??"

I couldn't stop the snicker that came out of me. Cori shot me a frown, and I covered my mouth.

"He's a good guy," she said. "He listens, he's supportive, and, yes, he has grown into his features." She sounded like she was rattling off a grocery list. Cori didn't speak about Nick with the same wonder that she had when she talked about Janet.

"Barf. Cooties. Are you in love with him?" Sam asked, his tongue sticking out. I was waiting for Cori to say that she was. Instead, she dropped her head into her hands and started to cry. She covered her face. "Whoa, Cori, I'm sorry." Sam turned to me, brow furrowed with worry. "What did I say?" he asked.

My impulse was to go over to her and hug her, but the awkwardness of the years between us stopped me. After a painful minute, her body relaxed, and she dropped her hands from her face, the mascara underneath her left eye smudged. She took a deep breath and then let out a laugh. I was with Sam: nothing Cori had said or done in the last minute made any kind of sense.

"I didn't mean to—" Sam started, but she held up her hand.

"You didn't do anything wrong," Cori said with a small grin. "This time." She wiped the tears from her cheek. "There are a few things I need to figure out." Cori turned to me. "Can you help him rinse his hair in eight minutes?" I nodded and she walked out of the bathroom, the familiar smell of the coconut shampoo Tiffany used to use wafting by me.

"I bet Nick is still a dick," Sam said.

I had a feeling it was more complicated than that.

❧ ❧ ❧

Sam jumped on Tiffany's old bed like he was trying to break it. He wore his new red pajamas, his now-blond hair flopping up and down, the bed squeaking with every hop.

"Can you believe we're in here?" Sam asked with glee. "Tiffany would have *hated* this!"

I put a glass of water on the nightstand. There were photos of Tiffany and her friends and a can of Aqua Net on the dresser, a poster of George Michael on the wall, her high school diploma framed above her vanity mirror, and a clock radio that blinked 12:00 that nobody bothered to fix.

"It's time for bed," I said, sounding like my dad when Nilou was up too late.

Sam stopped jumping. "Aw, come on. I'm not even tired."

"Yeah, but I am." Cori was, too. Sam shrugged and pulled back the comforter, settling himself under the sheets. I tucked him in. "Try and get some sleep. We'll figure everything out in the morning."

"What's to figure out?" Sam asked.

"You know, how to keep you away from people who might recognize you. Where you're going to live. You can't stay here forever," I said. "I'm going to college in the fall. I don't know which school yet, but I can get an apartment and you can stay with me."

"A life reset!"

"Yeah! It'll be great!"

"We can do whatever we want? Stay up all night and watch R-rated movies?"

I already could see R-rated movies, but I appreciated the enthusiasm.

"We'll make our own rules," I agreed. I hesitated before I forced myself to continue. "Sam, about this afternoon. At the arcade. When all the games were going haywire . . . did you do that?"

Sam stared at me for a few moments. His face expressionless, his eyes blank, as though he were a battery-operated toy that had run out of juice. "It wasn't me," he said.

"You sure? You didn't do anything to that kid?"

"I'm trying not to hurt anybody," he murmured, looking down at the paisley-patterned comforter. It wasn't a denial. He lifted his head. "You believe me, right?"

We stared at each other. I couldn't give him the answer he wanted. I stood up and walked to the doorway, my hand on the light switch.

"I think it's been a long day and there's a lot we have to work out. The three of us, together."

Sam nodded, wiggling into a more comfortable position.

"Maz? Could you keep the hall light on for a while?" Even after all this time, he was still a little spooked by the dark. Then again, for him no time had passed at all.

22

HOW COULD I APPROACH JANET without sounding like a complete idiot? I had half a mind to go to her now, even with Sam in the house, but maybe she needed a little space? I wouldn't even know what to say. What if she wanted more from me than I was able to give? I couldn't ask her to homecoming, but we could try going on a date out of town. What would that even look like? Had we been dating this whole time anyway? I never cared about being a good girlfriend to Nick, but what if I was bad at a relationship I really wanted?

"He's all tucked in," Maz said as he lumbered down the stairs. I had just finished making a bed for him on the sofa.

"You sure you don't want to sleep in my parents' room?" I asked. Maz shook his head. Potato Chip was curled up on the rug in front of the TV, blissfully unaware of the mess that was my life.

"It was already a trip being in Tiffany's," Maz said, sitting down on top of the sheets. I sat in the armchair. "It's surreal even being in your living room."

"I bet," I said. Before we had a chance to lapse into awkward silence, I asked, "How's Nilou?"

"Almost a teenager," Maz said with a smile.

"God, she is, isn't she? What's she like?"

"She's still curious and fun-loving, but now she has attitude. She's one of the *cool* girls at school."

"I'm not surprised. She's always been the coolest member of your family."

"She would be over the moon excited to see you again. So would my parents."

I had thought of the Shahzad family over the years, especially Mrs. Shahzad. She'd always been so kind to me and still sent us a store-bought card around the holidays. I'd send one back, but neither of us ever sent family photos or extensive updates. I was curious to know how they were all doing.

"I'd like to come by and see everyone. If that's all right with you?" I asked.

"It's always been all right with me." He looked away. It shouldn't be this weird to talk to someone I once knew like the back of my hand.

"I'm sorry I let so much time go by," I whispered. "I was scared."

"I was, too. You're not anymore?"

"I'm scared of lots of things," I answered honestly. "Mostly of myself." We were doing okay so far. I didn't think I'd want to unload my burgeoning sapphic identity crisis on him, but he was Maz, and even after all this time my instinct was to tell him everything.

"You are pretty terrifying," Maz said, his small smile growing wider. "I will say this for Sam, he knows how to tear us apart, but he also knows how to bring us together." There was a pause so pregnant that it was about to go into labor.

"What are we going to do?" I whispered. "I mean, if this pinball machine can really *take* people? How do we stop it?"

"Maybe it's like the game in that movie *The Last Starfighter*? You know how it recruits troops for battle."

If this was the best we could come up with, we were doomed. *We* were supposed to be the adults here. "Who would recruit Sam to save their solar system?"

"All I know is someone or something took him for a reason." Unless the machine is like the car in *Christine*, evil and bloodthirsty for no reason. "He's going to be okay, right? I mean, he seems fine. Mostly." I focused on the *mostly*.

"Have you noticed anything weird? I mean, other than the not aging?"

"No," Maz answered, a little too quickly for my liking. "There was this thing at the mall, but it looked worse than it was."

"What thing?"

Maz clasped his hands together in between his knees. "We went into the arcade and this kid was being a jerk and wanted the game we were playing. Then the games went berserk, like turned off and on all at once, and the kid fell to the ground choking." I blinked at him, my mouth hanging open. "It all worked out!" he said. "The kid was okay! I don't think Sam did it on purpose!"

"You're only telling me this now?" I asked him, incredulous.

He should have told me as soon as he got home. "How do you know Sam *didn't mean to do it*?"

"Because he told me," Maz said. It was slowly dawning on me that *I* was the only adult in the room. "I mean, he said he wasn't trying to hurt anybody."

"And you believed him?" I shouted before I remembered Sam could probably hear us. I lowered my voice to an angry whisper. "You don't think there's some correlation between a boy returning from the inside of an arcade game and then causing havoc at an arcade?"

Maz deflated into the couch and wiped his palms on the legs of his jeans. "Well, sure, when you put it that way," he said. "So what do we do?"

"You think I know what to do in this situation?" I asked. "You think I can speed-dial a priest to perform a pinball exorcism? Jeez, Maz." I rubbed my temples with my index fingers. I realized it was something Mom did when she listened to Tiffany complain about Brooks, so I stopped, tucking my hands under my legs. "Even if we find the *Sorcerer* machine, what do you expect me to do? Shove Sam back in the coin slot?"

"What if we destroyed it?" Maz asked. "Maybe it would make Sam normal again?"

"Or it could cause him and everyone else he claims to be in there to be lost forever." If it were that easy to fix, it wouldn't be a problem.

Maz sank even deeper into the couch. "I don't want to lose him again," he said. "I know he's not quite the same, but it's not his fault. Something did this *to* him. And we had so much fun today, Cori. I didn't even want a dri—" He stopped himself. "It was like old times. The good times."

I didn't know what Maz had been up to the past few years, but I remembered the way he turned inward after Sam disappeared. He'd kept to himself. He stayed close to home. I was glad to see he was with a friend when I saw him that day at the mall, and from his jacket I could tell he was a team captain, but maybe he hadn't had an easy time in high school. Who was I kidding? *No one* had an easy time in high school.

"I want to help him, too. But we have to be practical. You have to stop pretending everything is awesome and meet me halfway and admit that he's . . . that we don't know everything that we should about him. We don't know what happened to him and we don't know what he is capable of."

I was gearing up to argue more when a car honked outside. Maz yelped. Headlights shone through the window as the horn blared again. Potato Chip was on his hind legs, yipping at the door, his tail wagging. I went to the front door and opened it a sliver to look outside.

Nick got out of his friend Adam's car and strolled up to Maz's in the driveway. "You have got to be kidding me." I groaned. I put my shoes on and opened the door more. "If Sam comes downstairs, make sure he stays inside." Adam sat behind the wheel, the windows of his car down. On the radio the Beastie Boys chanted, "Whatcha want." I was so tired of boys, beastie or otherwise. I wanted them all to grow the hell up. Tim got out of the car and sat on the trunk, a six-pack of Natty Light resting on his knee.

"What is this, Nick? It's eleven o'clock." I didn't have the energy for the sickly sweet fare I usually served him. Instead, my voice was normal. I sounded like *me*.

"Whose car is this?" he asked. He smelled like a mixture of Jovan Musk, flop sweat, stale beer, and Cool Ranch Doritos. Janet smelled better even when she reeked of ammonia from the fixer in the photo lab.

"You've had quite a night," I said, wrapping my arms around myself. The air was damp and chilly, a mist forming as though it were about to rain.

"We won the game." Nick's body drooped and his eyelids looked heavy. He swayed as he stood. "I wanted to celebrate with you, but you were gone. Vickie said you left with Maz, your friend from elementary school?"

"He had a family emergency."

"Is that his car?" Nick asked, more impressed than hurt. He teetered toward me. "I wanted my girlfriend to be there for me."

"I'm glad you won," I said. "We can celebrate some other time, but tonight isn't going to work."

"It was so embarrassing having the guys from the team ask where you were and I didn't know."

I waved to Adam and Tim, who were still his best friends but not his teammates. They weren't so bad, so long as they didn't talk.

"I was right here, guys!" I shouted at them. "Nothing to worry your pretty little heads about." I met Nick's eyes. "Please leave. We'll talk when you're sober."

Nick took a step back, but he was still playing the tough guy.

"How long have you been keeping me on hold for, huh? I've been patient. I haven't complained about just making out and not going all the way. I mean, we've been going out a few months, like, what is up?"

If my head could have exploded like a volcano, with hot magma oozing down my temples, burning my flesh and the earth below my feet, it still would not be enough to show him how furious I was. Nick looked at me like I had transformed from Dr. Jekyll to Mr. Hyde.

"Nick." I struggled to keep my voice calm. "Other than my looks, what is it that you like about me?"

With his forehead furrowed and his mouth agape, he was searching his innermost thoughts and feelings and failing right before my eyes. "You're . . . you're not like any of the other girls," he said finally, with drunken confidence. He closed his mouth, a hint of a smile on his lips, thinking he had said exactly the right thing.

I abhorred the expression *not like other girls*. I had spent my whole life trying to *be* like the other girls. I tried to look and behave a way that was considered "feminine" and "mainstream." I made sure I never came across as too smart. I kept keeping my opinions to myself. I spent years pretending to like things girls my age were supposed to like, including fashion, the musical stylings of Marky Mark and the Funky Bunch, and, of course, boys. I actually had nothing in common with the girls I hung out with at school. It didn't make them bad people, but it also didn't make them better than me or the right kind of girl. And then I realized it. None of us were ever going to be enough. We would be ranked, scrutinized, courted, insulted, praised, objectified, and observed by men our entire lives. How they saw us determined our value. We'd never win the game if we kept playing by their damn rules.

"I can't be the girlfriend you'd like me to be," I said loud and clear so there wouldn't be any misunderstanding. "I'm breaking up with you, Nick. No hard feelings. I hope the rest of the season goes well for you and the team."

I walked back toward the house.

"But what about homecoming?" he yelled.

I slammed the door behind me. Sam and Maz stood next to each other in the foyer. Maz looked a little gray.

"Some guys can't hold their booze, I guess," Maz said softly, his eyes wide like he was processing something.

"I knew he was still a dick," Sam said with satisfaction.

23

SAM

SEPTEMBER 27, 1992

I'M HUNGRY. It's hungry.

Sam.

I didn't wake my friends. They don't need to know.

You are not doing what you have been asked to do.

Shut up. You're not my mom. Don't pretend anymore. I know you.

You prefer my real voice? Fine. There. Is this better?

Ugh, gross. You sound so old and boring.

How charming. Sam, you have not made any progress.

Yeah, well, I want to have some fun first. Spend time with my friends. Oh sorry, that's probably a word you don't know. A *friend* is someone who cares about you and wants to hang out with you without having to pay for their company.

I do know what happens the longer you prolong your stay. Do you?

Yeah, yeah. I have to feed the machine. What do you think I'm doing out here in the middle of the night?

I know that you aren't doing what I commanded you to do.

It bugs you that I'm taking my sweet time, doesn't it? I'm out in the real world and you're stuck in there. Fine by me, you old fart.

Call me all the names you like, but your time is running out.

Don't you mean your time is running out?

. . .

No answer for that, huh?

My patience is wearing thin.

Like your hair?

Enough! Do what I have tasked you to do. Quickly.

Okay, okay. I will. But not because I like you.

I am comfortable with not being liked. Are you?

My friends like me.

Do they? Will they after they know?

. . .

Who is the silent one now?

Shut up. I have to concentrate. I see him, but he doesn't see me.

Fine. But remember—

You're waiting, it's very important, blah, blah, blah. Give it a rest.

Good boy.

◖ ◖ ◖

I see him sitting on one of the risers looking out at the football field. Hoo-doggy is he loaded! And crying! Oh man, oh man, this is priceless. I can't believe his friends left him alone here.

"Adam?" he asks, then wipes his face quickly. Guess he doesn't want his pals to know he's a crybaby.

"Hey, Nick the Dick."

"What?" Nick's floppy and wobbly, but the closer I get, the more he straightens up. His eyes bug out when he recognizes me. "Sam? What was in that beer?"

"No, I'm really here."

"You're dead." He sounds so confident when he says it. "I must be really drunk."

"You are! But not *that* drunk!"

He licks his lips and squints. I guess he's going to need some convincing.

"You remember when you pegged me with that dodgeball in fourth grade during gym?" I ask. "You kept going after me, but you made it look like you weren't? I mean, you and I knew, but everybody else thought you were playing an ordinary game."

Now he is getting it. His eyes work overtime with lots of blinking.

"You made my nose bleed. But I didn't cry. I guess that always kind of bugged you, huh? That you couldn't really get to me. So, you gave me a cute little name. Sam the Squirt. Are you still that clever or have the head injuries made you a little dumber now?"

I could tell he was deciding whether he should scream, or run, or fight me, but his body wasn't going to let him do any of that. Not now that he was in my sights.

"I promise, this won't hurt as much as getting hit by a dodgeball. Well, okay, it'll hurt a lot more than that, but it won't last long if you stay still."

I begin to eat. I feed the machine.

24.

CORI

I WOKE UP TO POTATO CHIP LICKING MY FACE. I'd brought him into my room for the night so he wouldn't bother Maz downstairs. I'd also locked my bedroom door. I'd like to say it was because I hadn't wanted Potato Chip to push it open in the middle of the night, but it was mostly so Sam couldn't get in. I'd felt guilty about it, but not enough to forgo protecting myself.

When I made it downstairs, the sounds of cartoons and Sam laughing drifted in from the living room. Maz was in the kitchen cooking breakfast.

"How'd you sleep?" Maz asked me as he scrambled eggs.

"Not well," I said honestly.

"Sam! Breakfast is ready!"

I heard the pitter-patter of feet and felt my spine tingle.

"Morning!" Sam bounced to his seat. "Isn't it a glorious day?"

I didn't think it was possible, but he seemed more energetic than he had been the day before.

"Someone's peppy. Did you give him coffee?" I asked Maz as I walked to get some myself.

"No," Sam answered. "I don't want to stunt my growth."

I didn't laugh.

"Oh, come on! That deserves a giggle."

Was it even possible for him to grow?

I didn't join Sam at the table. Instead, I sipped my coffee leaning next to the sink. Maz put a plate of food in front of Sam.

"Thanks," Sam said, but he didn't dig in.

Maz brought two more plates to the table and sat down. I took another sip of coffee. I let my mind wander until Maz asked, "What do you think, Cori?"

"About what?" I hadn't been listening.

"I can pick Sam up before school tomorrow and take him to a movie." I wasn't sure it was the best idea to leave Sam alone anywhere, but I would be relieved to have him out of my house.

"Sam," I said, avoiding Maz's question. "When the machine let you out, where was it?"

"This again," Sam said, rolling his eyes. "It was in a basement somewhere. It was too dark, I couldn't see."

A basement. At least that was something.

"Okay, was it the basement of a store? Do you remember the neighborhood or street?"

"Nope. I was kind of out of it. It's all a bit foggy."

"Cori, eat before your food gets cold."

"Tell him to do the same," I snapped. Sam hadn't touched his eggs. He hadn't eaten any of the pizza we ordered last night either. Maz stopped chewing, glancing at Sam's plate. He swallowed slowly.

"You didn't eat at the food court yesterday," he said, worry in his voice instead of the judgment in mine.

"I don't have much of an appetite for food," Sam said. "But maybe it'll come back."

Maz and I looked at each other. As Maz said last night, none of this was Sam's fault. And yet, it didn't help the sinking feeling I had that Sam was never supposed to come back. That, perhaps, I didn't want him to come back.

"I've got to make an appearance at home today. My parents thought I spent the night at Derek's. I tried to call him to cover for me in case they called, but your phone wasn't working," Maz said as he pushed his plate of unfinished eggs to the side. "Are you two going to be okay together?"

I took a sip of coffee, avoiding eye contact with Sam, taking in his pajamas. Sam might have come back broken, or messed up, but he was still a kid. I sat down at the table with them. Sam beamed at me.

"We'll be fine," I said.

❧ ❧ ❧

"You sunk my battleship. Again," I muttered.

"You bet your ass I did!" Sam exclaimed. We had also played Connect 4, checkers, and the Game of Life in the span of a few hours. I was exhausted, but this was the price I paid for not letting Sam go outside. "Want to play again?"

"I think I could use a break." I hadn't played any of these games in years, and I would be happy to go another five or ten before playing them again. "How about I put on a movie?" Sam's exuberance dimmed a little. "Nothing scary," I quickly added.

"Okay!" He rubbed his hands together. I looked at our shelf of VHS tapes underneath the TV. I had to skip over a lot of my favorites so all I was left with were movies my parents liked. I picked *Field of Dreams*; the only thing scary about it was that it made my dad tear up at the end.

"You'll like this one," I said, pushing the tape into the VCR. Sam and I sat on opposite sides of the couch.

"Do you think we could rent some of the movies I missed?" Sam asked. "Maybe next weekend?" I couldn't even think about Sam staying here for another week. Would I have to babysit him for the rest of my life? "Maz said there are six *Police Academy* movies."

"We're not watching those." Sam grinned. I hadn't realized he was joking. "You're a riot."

"It's nice seeing you smile," he said. "You haven't done a lot of it since I've been back."

I looked down at my lap, the smile waning.

"It's okay, I get it. It's weird. But I'm still me, Cori."

After staring at my knees for what felt like an eternity, I raised my head to look at Sam. His eyes were squeezed shut, but tears poured out of them anyway. I reached over and put my hand on his shoulder. It was the first time I'd touched him.

"I've lost a lot of time," he whispered. "I've lost a lot."

I pulled him close to me and hugged him. He cried on my shoulder. I held him through all of his whimpers and sobs. I had done this so many times before.

"I'm here."

25.

CORI

MR. BENNETT OPENED THE DOOR to the apartment.

"Hi," he said. He looked so incredibly sad. "Thanks so much for coming." At eight years old, I didn't quite understand the magnitude of the situation. Mom only told me that Sam needed a friend and that Mrs. Bennett was away.

I looked up at Mr. Bennett. He was tall and thin and let us eat cereal whenever we wanted, even for dinner. He was a weird dad, but that was okay because Sam loved him and I loved Sam.

"Can I see him?" I asked.

"'May I,'" Mom corrected, still holding my hand.

"Please. He won't come out," Mr. Bennett said. I walked to Sam's room. "Can I get you something to drink?" he asked my mom.

"No thank you," she replied. She didn't correct his grammar.

I knocked on Sam's door. It was still covered in the brightly colored scratch-and-sniff stickers that we put up on it, but they'd lost their scent a long time ago.

"Sam. I'm here," I said to the door.

"I don't know what I'm going to do now that Cynthia's gone," Mr. Bennett said, in the kitchen.

I pushed the door open. Sam was sitting on the floor, reading an Archie comic, or staring at an Archie comic. He didn't say hello, but he didn't tell me to go away, either. I sat across from him. He passed me a comic book. I liked Sabrina fine, so I flipped through looking for her. When all I got was Josie and the Pussycats, I pretended like I was still interested.

"She might come back," Sam said. I looked up, but he was still staring down at Jughead eating a burger. "When she does, I'll be better."

I knew I should say that she might, but I couldn't. Sam's mom always looked tired, the kind of tired like she was living someone else's life. I knew she was never coming back.

I scooched right next to Sam and put my arm around his shoulder.

26.

MAZ

"BREATHE IN THROUGH YOUR NOSE, out your mouth,"
Coach Gillis said as we sat on the grass with our eyes closed.
He was having us visualize what we wanted the race against
Armstead to look like. He started doing this last season and we
used to think it was dumb, but there is something to it. Except
every time we had a race against Armstead, the visualizations
got longer and longer. We already went through our drills. Butt
kicks, skips, back striders, leg swings, bounding—nothing
we couldn't handle. I went through the motions, but I was
thinking about Sam and Cori. I couldn't sleep over again on a
weeknight, my parents wouldn't go for that, but they thought
I would be at Coach's for his team dinner, so I had until about
eight thirty.

"Remember we've got the advantage. They're going to be on
our home turf. They don't know the course like you do. They
don't know the sweat and passion and effort you've got inside of
you. Think about how you're going to show them."

Where was I going to stash Sam once Cori's parents came back to town? Today I'd left him at the movie theater. *Honey, I Blew Up the Kid* was still playing, and it had a 10:30 a.m. showing. I bought two tickets, one so I could get in, a giant tub of popcorn, Milk Duds, and a large soda, even though I was pretty sure he wasn't going to eat any of it. I told him not to leave the multiplex until I came to get him after practice. I'd missed two of my morning classes but made it to school in time for my history test. If I could get out of the team dinner tonight, I could pick up Sam and take him to Cori's.

"The finish line is closer than you think," Coach said, signaling the end of the visualization. "All right, let's line up, gentlemen. Twenty-minute tempo run around campus."

I opened my eyes and saw Coach Gillis's daughter, Cleo, sitting on a bench reading a book. She was often a guest at our practices, tuning out her dad's lectures and our panting while finishing up her homework. She was shy and I had a soft spot for her, mostly because her round face reminded me a little of Cori's when we were younger.

"Let's go, guys!" Derek said.

I joined him up front, leading the boys off the track and toward the soccer fields. I kept up with Derek as we started with a light jog. Once we passed the soccer fields and got to the football field, Derek picked up speed.

"Push it," he shouted, setting our pace.

"Push it real good," I yelled, and that got some wheezy chuckles. Brewster, a sophomore, kept in step with me on my right. When we went up the hill toward the science building, most of us started to jog again, but Brewster kept his pace, pushing ahead of Derek and me.

"Slow it down, rookie," Derek called, but Brewster ignored him. I went faster and the group followed me. "Turn it down!"

I slowed because Derek told me to, but Brewster looked over his shoulder and flashed us a grin. The little twerp!

"Looks like we've got a challenge!" Paul yelled, egging Brewster on. The team cheered as I went full speed, catching up quickly.

"Get him, Maz!" Quincy shouted. Derek and the rest of the team stayed behind as Brewster and I jockeyed for position.

"I'm going for top five," Brewster said in between pants. The last thing I needed was for this kid to take the place of one of our seniors—or even me—in a race. I know, there's no *I* in *team*, but there's also no college admissions committee ignoring my occasional C in lieu of my excellent racing ability if I'm not the best on the team.

"That a fact?" I asked. I stayed close to him, arms out front, focused on my breathing. We climbed up the hill, raced past the main schoolhouse and auditorium, then descended down the parking lot and headed back to the track. From the corner of my eye, I could see Brewster struggling. I turned on the jets and tore past him, not looking back, charging toward home base.

I neared the bleachers.

"Hey, Maz!" There was a shock of blond hair that got my attention. Sam gave me a cheerful wave. I didn't slow down until I reached the bench where he sat with Cleo.

"What—" I started, trying to catch my breath. "What are you doing here?" I turned my head to find Brewster and the rest of the team heading our way.

"I got bored," Sam said with a shrug. "I'm happy that the kid gets really tall, but I mean it's, like, in the title and poster, you know? Where's the suspense?"

I glanced over at Cleo. Her book, which was usually all she focused on during practice, was tossed on top of her backpack. I wondered what they'd been talking about.

"We better get going." I took Sam by the hand and lifted him off the bench just as the rest of the team reached the track.

"Practice isn't over yet," Coach Gillis said, coming over to us before I could get Sam to the locker room. "Friend of yours?"

"I know," I gasped, hoping Coach thought I was trying to catch my breath instead of stalling for time. "This is Peter." Coach Gillis stared at us, waiting for more of an explanation. I struggled to remember the excuse I'd given Janet. "I'm his Big Brother. Part of my community service requirement." We had to have fifty hours of volunteer work completed before we graduated. I'd finished mine freshman year volunteering at my dad's hospital, dropping off water and newspapers in patients' rooms and delivering urine and blood samples to the lab, but Coach didn't know that.

"That's great." Coach's voice was completely flat. "Peter can wait here with Cleo until practice is over."

Sam beamed. Cleo blushed and glanced sheepishly at him.

"Do you think it'd be okay if Peter came over with Maz tonight?" Cleo asked.

"Oh yeah! Cleo invited me! Isn't that cool?" He had managed to charm my coach's daughter in less than half an hour.

"I think that'll be fine," Coach Gillis said. "This gives Maz an opportunity to rack up more of those community service hours, right?"

"What's wrong with you?" I heard Derek say to Brewster as the team all staggered toward us. "Save that for the race. You too, Maz." He turned to me, then looked down at Sam by my side. "Who's the kid?" Derek huffed.

"This is Maz's friend Peter, from the Big Brothers Big Sisters program," Coach said to the team. "He'll be joining us tonight."

"Since when did you start mentoring?" Derek asked me, his eyebrows raised in either delighted surprise or disbelief, I couldn't tell which.

"Recently," I said, trying not to look suspicious as I glanced at the team. Was there anyone here who would recognize Sam?

"I can't believe someone would trust you to be responsible for their kid," Derek said before he winked at Sam and pointed a finger at him. "Hi, Peter. I'm Derek. How's it going, little man?"

"Fine so long as you don't call me *little man* ever again." Sam winked and pointed back at Derek.

"Cute kid," Derek said to me with a hint of annoyance.

Sam watched him a little too fixedly for my liking.

27.

CORI

I HAD BEEN PREPARED for people at school to whisper about my breakup with Nick, but I didn't expect them to look at me like a member of my family had just died. I was used to attention, but today it felt like I was getting way more than my usual share. Walking down the hallway, I kept an eye out for Janet, hoping to find a moment to talk to her.

"Hey, Cori," Samantha Weller from the cheerleading team called to me in a soft, cooing voice. "How are you holding up?"

"Fine," I said. Why was everyone acting so weird?

"We're all pulling for Nick," Samantha said, trailed by some other girls from the team who gave me a nod. Hold up, *Nick*? Where was the solidarity? Shouldn't she be "pulling" for me? After I hit my locker, I would go straight to Janet's. Gossip traveled so fast, but if I had a chance, I wanted to tell Janet that I was single myself.

Before I even got to my locker, Vickie ran to me and gave me the biggest, longest hug in the history of our friendship.

"Are you okay?" she asked. Her hair hid my face, but I could see everyone in the hallway watching us in between the strands.

"I think so," I said. She let go of me, but stayed close, looping her arm in mine. I didn't think my relationship with Nick meant so much to the entire school. "People seem to be taking the breakup harder than I am."

"What breakup?" Vickie asked me. I noticed her eyes were red and puffy. Had she been crying over this?

"I dumped Nick," I said. She blinked at me like I was speaking a foreign language. Then her face fell.

"You don't know, do you?" She pulled me by my arm and led me into the bathroom. There were three girls in there, one washing her hands, and the other two, from Janet's circle, were checking their reflections in the mirror. Their faces turned sullen at the sight of me. "Out," Vickie commanded, and they all left without protest.

"Vickie, you're starting to freak me out."

She fell into my arms and shook against me. She mumbled something into my shoulder, but I couldn't understand what she was saying. I rubbed circles on her back to calm her down.

"What's wrong?" I asked.

"Nick is in the hospital."

"What?" I started to feel sick. "Did he get in a car accident?"

"No," she whimpered, backing away from me a little, mascara running down her cheeks. "The grounds crew found him on the football field. They didn't know what was wrong with him, he was just lying there, totally out of it."

"Is he dead?" I asked, my chest tight.

"No, but I guess he's, like, in a coma or something." I had to see Nick as soon as I could.

"I tried calling you, but I kept getting this weird static."

❧ ❧ ❧

The sterile hallways in the ICU were eerily quiet. Staff sat at the main desk, and in the rooms, a few nurses checked in on patients behind curtains. I had my guest sticker on, but I still felt out of place. I wasn't sure what you got for your ex-boyfriend who was in a coma, but I figured roses from the gift shop were a safe bet.

The door to room 2B was open; Mrs. Dawson sat vigil by Nick's bed. He was hooked up to monitors, the kind that beeped every couple of seconds to let you know things were holding steady. I expected him to be asleep, but his eyes were wide open, as though he were staring right at me. His mouth, which was covered with an oxygen mask, looked like it was stuck in a scream.

"Cori." Mrs. Dawson got up from her plastic chair and greeted me in the doorway. She was generally a cheerful woman. Always involved in a bake sale, a bit nosy, but never maliciously so. She still rocked a mom mullet, but it suited her. Now the mullet was in a disheveled ponytail and she looked like she hadn't slept in years.

"I just heard," I said, hugging her even though I couldn't take my eyes off of Nick. "I'm so sorry."

"They tried to tape his eyes shut, but nothing works." She started crying.

"What happened?" I asked.

Mrs. Dawson let me go, took a deep breath, and sat back down. I watched Nick as I leaned over to put the flowers on his bedside table.

"He didn't come home Saturday night. Mr. Dawson and I were a little worried, but we figured after the big win, he was still with his friends. By Sunday afternoon, when he still wasn't home, we started calling folks. I called you, but it never rang. I just got static. Was your phone off the hook?"

"We lost power for a while on Sunday," I lied. I had a feeling whatever was "wrong" with the phones was thanks to Sam.

"We finally got a hold of Adam, and he said the last time he saw Nick was when he dropped him off at the football field. They'd been drinking, I don't know how they *got* beer. I bet it's that Tim's fault. He's such a bad influence. I called the school and the maintenance crew found him, faceup on the field, lying on his back just like this. The paramedics tried to close his eyes and mouth, but they just won't." She leaned over and pushed Nick's eyelids down, but as soon as her fingers pulled away, they bounced back open. "See? My beautiful boy won't talk or move. And nobody can explain it. The kids ask me when Nick will be back and I break down and cry."

I thought about Nick's three little siblings, all under ten. They weren't here now, but that was probably for the best. If I saw Tiffany like this, I wouldn't be able to sleep for years, and I didn't even like her all that much.

"The doctors say his vitals are good, and I'm grateful for that. But he hasn't moved or blinked . . . nothing. It's like he's . . . he's stuck."

I kept staring at Nick. What had he seen that left him frozen in abject horror? Was he still seeing it?

"I'm so glad you're here, Cori. He talks about you all the time. Cori said this or Cori said that. He thinks you're perfect." I bit my lower lip, guilt flooding my insides. I hadn't thought the same of him, and now he was here. I didn't want things to end with that fight.

"Would you try talking to him for a while?" Mrs. Dawson said. "The nurses say sometimes it helps to do that with coma patients, though we aren't sure if this is a regular coma."

"It's the least I can do," I said.

"I'm going to call the kids and make sure the babysitter can stay a little longer. I'll be right back." Mrs. Dawson slipped quietly out of the room.

I took a few steps forward and sat in her chair. It was still warm.

"Nick, can you hear me?" I asked, even though I felt stupid doing it. It's not like he could respond. "I'm sorry this happened to you." The monitors continued to beep steadily. It was the only sound for a while until I mustered up the courage to ask him what I needed to know. "Did you see a kid? White, bleached blond hair, four feet eight inches?" Nick didn't respond. I leaned in closer to whisper in his ear. "Did you see Sam Bennett?"

When I backed away, I saw a lone tear drip down the side of his unblinking eye.

❧ ❧ ❧

I leaned against the wall next to the pay phone in the hospital lobby. I didn't know if calling was the right thing to do. I'd picked up and put down the receiver three times. I felt unsteady, like my knees would give out at any second. The acid in my stomach threatened to come up my throat. I wish I dealt with stress the way Tiffany did. She would lash out, shout, never shy away from an argument, and I was exactly the opposite. She always took up all the emotional space in a room, leaving none for me. There were a lot of qualities my sister had that I had no interest in emulating, but I could see the benefits of oversharing once in a while.

I took the phone off the cradle one more time and pushed my coin through the slot. I knew the number by heart.

"Hello?" Her voice sounded strained. It made me wish I'd called sooner.

"I broke up with Nick," I said. "Now he's in the hospital. I know that's not because we broke up, but I feel bad about it. He's in a coma and nobody knows how to help him. His mom is really sweet, but she'll probably hate me when she finds out. He might not ever recover." My voice was thick with tears, but I kept going. "But I never feel bad when I'm with you. I'll never feel bad about wanting to be with you. I can't promise that I'll shout that from the rooftops, and you don't have to say anything, but I need you to know that you were right. I like you. And I'll never feel bad about that."

I tried to slow my breathing, choking back tears and hiding my face from strangers with my hand. The longer the silence on the other end, the longer I worried she didn't feel the same way anymore. I'd blown it. I was about to hang up when she finally spoke.

"Where are you?"

"I'm at the hospital, but I'm headed home. Should be there in twenty minutes."

"I'll meet you there."

❧ ❧ ❧

Janet beat me to my house. She was sitting on the front steps as I pulled into my driveway. I wished I had time to reapply my makeup. I must have looked a mess.

"Hey," Janet said, standing up as I got out of my car. She was wearing sweatpants and a Soundgarden T-shirt, one of her scuffed-up Chucks toeing the crumbling asphalt of the first step. My chest swelled the closer I got to her. "I'm sorry about Nick."

"Thanks," I said.

Her warm brown eyes gleamed in the dimming sunlight. She reached up to touch my face but thought better of it, looking past me. I realized she was trying to see if there were any neighbors around. I knew she was doing that for my benefit.

I put my arms around her, held her to me tightly, and felt her arms wrap around my waist.

"I was afraid to tell you," I whispered.

She gave me a squeeze before she let me go. "You think I wasn't?" she asked with a small laugh, wiping at her face as a few tears squeaked out. I'd never seen her cry before. "I like you better than anyone else. And I generally don't like all that many people!" We both giggled. "Ugh, feelings are a major energy suck."

"Tell me about it." I fished for the house keys in my purse. "We should eliminate all of them," I joked, unlocking the door and inviting her in. "I feel like it's a chamomile tea kind of day. It's pretty soothing."

"Soothing I can go for," she said, following me into the kitchen. I filled the kettle with water and joined her at the table while we waited for it to boil. "Is he going to be okay?"

"I hope so." I felt heavy. There was no amount of tea that was going to revive me. "You know Donald Sutherland's face at the end of *Invasion of the Body Snatchers* when he screams?" Janet nodded because of course she did. She was the only person who got every reference I made. "Nick's face was like that."

"Whoa." She sounded part sympathetic, part fascinated. I could tell she wanted to ask me more. "I mean, I know you're a heartbreaker, but that's an intense reaction."

"That's not funny."

"I know. Sorry. I'm nervous I guess." Janet blushed. "I'm not sure how to do this."

"Do what?" The kettle began to whistle, but I didn't move. I wanted to hear this.

She took a moment, staring at the table instead of at me.

"The timing's off. I feel like our timing is always off. I don't want Nick to be hurt or anything. I know I should be comforting you about him, but I also want to kiss you and that feels so not the right thing to do now because, you know, he's body-snatched or whatever."

I looked at her sheepishly, then turned to take the kettle off the stove. "But lately I've come to find that time is kind of a lie," I said.

I turned back around, reached across the table, and touched her hand. She opened her palm to me, and my stomach fluttered when she brushed her thumb over mine. "I am looking forward to the kissing though. Once things are a little less sad," I said.

"I am too," she said.

Thinking about it made my skin hot.

"Forget tea. I should probably take Potato Chip out on his walk. Come with me?" I pulled her up and hugged her again.

"Still too sad?" Janet asked, and I laughed. She let go and cleared her throat, but her cheeks were rosy and I really, *really*, loved that shade on her. "Potato Chip! Where are you?" There was no sign of him. We went upstairs, calling out his name. He didn't make a peep. I checked my room and the upstairs bathroom, but I couldn't find him.

Then I heard Janet scream, "Cori!"

I rushed to Tiffany's room. Janet pointed a trembling finger to the bed.

"He's under there." Her lip quivered as she told me.

I had been dreading this day for a while. He was getting older, but I thought we'd have at least another year or so. He'd been with me through so much, and I wasn't ready to say goodbye. He was such a good boy. *My* good boy. I dropped down and crawled under the bed, tears already pouring out of me.

The dog that I had had since I was a kid was standing on four legs, snarling with his teeth bared, his tail and ears sticking up in the air. Potato Chip didn't make any noise, didn't move, didn't breathe.

My dog was a statue that was not meant to be on display.

28.

MAZ

SEPTEMBER 28, 1992

"WHY SHOULD YOU NEVER TRUST A BIG BUTT and a smile?" Sam asked as we drove to Coach Gillis's house. The song on the radio was a little over his head.

"I'll tell you when you're a little older," I said, changing the station. An old Cars song, one of Sam's favorites, came on. He turned up the volume and sang along. "We're not going to stay long, okay?"

"I know, we've gone over it a kajillion times," Sam said. "*Peter* has to be home at a reasonable hour because his mom is waiting for him. What a crock of shit."

"Language."

"Are you kidding?"

I parked behind Derek's car. Ezra, Quincy, and Paul were all there already, their cars parked along the street near Coach's house. Craig and Brewster probably got a lift from somebody. I'd usually offer them a ride, but I figured the less time Sam spent with everybody, the better. He'd been pretty well behaved, waiting for me in the parking lot after I showered and changed. He'd been polite with everyone and nothing weird had happened. Cori should have been there. She needed to see that Sam wasn't as messed up as she thought he was.

"Okay, we say hello, eat, say thank you, and hope Coach doesn't make a speech, then get out of there."

I offered him a high five. We said "Buds" and then got out of the car and walked toward the house.

"What's with the whole . . . Alex P. Keaton vibe?" Sam said, looking me up and down. It took me a second to remember who Alex P. Keaton was. I laughed when I remembered the overzealous young Republican on *Family Ties*, who was always trying to make money and get ahead.

"We have a dress code at Carter."

"Okay. But we're not at Carter now and you're wearing boat shoes and khakis. What happened to high tops and jeans?"

"I wear those sometimes," I protested. "Besides, what's wrong with khakis?"

"Nothing, I guess." I saw him fidgeting out of the corner of my eye as we reached the door. I pushed the bell.

"Is it okay if *I'm* wearing jeans?"

Oh, he was worried he was underdressed. "You look great," I assured him. I should get him some more clothes.

Mrs. Gillis, a curvy white lady with a brunette bob haircut that hadn't changed since I'd started at Carter, greeted us. She worked in admissions at the Nichols School and always brought orange slices to our races. She looked so happy to see Sam, I would have thought he was the guest of honor.

"Hello, boys," Mrs. Gillis said.

"Hi, Mrs. G. Looking fabulous as always," I said, and felt Sam's eyes on me. "I'm sorry I came empty-handed. I hope it's okay that I brought my friend Peter along."

"I'm so glad you did! Peter, Cleo told me all about you as soon as she got home," Mrs. Gillis said, opening the door and waving us in with more enthusiasm than I had ever seen. I guess Cleo wasn't having the easiest time making friends. "The boys are out in the yard. It's still nice enough for a barbecue. I hope you like burgers, Peter!"

"Thank you," Sam said. He was as polite with Mrs. Gillis as he'd always been with my mom.

"You look so familiar," Mrs. Gillis said, studying Sam's face as we stood in her foyer. "Have we met before?"

My armpits started to go into sweat overdrive. We should make a run for it before she figured it out.

"No, but I'm glad we're meeting now," Sam said, sweet as could be. She ate it up with a spoon.

"I'll let Cleo know you're here! Make yourselves at home." Mrs. Gillis headed up the stairs, leaving us alone to go join the guys. Sam walked in step with me through the kitchen and out to the backyard. Coach was manning the grill with help from Quincy, flipping burgers and repositioning hot dogs.

"About time you showed up," Derek said, clasping my hand in a high five and bringing me in for a pat on the back. He turned to Sam. "This guy taking good care of you, Peter?"

Sam only nodded.

"Are you sure?" Paul asked, elbowing Ezra, who was in the lawn chair next to him. "If Maz starts giving you any tips on

how 'men are from Mars, women are from Venus,' don't listen."
I felt my face get hot. Stacey had given me a copy of the self-help
book three weeks before she dumped me. When the guys found
it in my locker, they took turns reading it aloud and goofing
on it.

"Is that sci-fi?" Sam asked.

The guys laughed.

"Might as well be, Pete," Ezra said, lying back in his chair. He
was one to talk. He actively avoided girls at parties and dances.
Derek reached into the cooler and pulled out a bottle of water.

"It's really cool that you and Maz are hanging out," he said,
handing Sam the drink. "Where do you go to school?"

"Aw, we don't want to bore Peter with small talk." I stood
between Derek and Sam. "Coach, do you have a Frisbee we can
toss around or something?"

"No Frisbee," Coach said. "But burgers are almost ready.
Peter, how do you like yours cooked?"

"I'm not very hungry, thank you," Sam said, his drink
unopened in his hand. "Don't want to spoil my appetite. Mom
has dinner waiting at home for me." He would have been pretty
convincing, except he shot me a look that basically said, *There,
are you satisfied?*

"Okay," Coach said. "Let me know if you change your mind."

Brewster and Craig brought the potato salad and corn on
the cob to the table from inside the house. Cleo followed them,
carrying a stack of paper plates, napkins, and a small box of
plastic silverware. She'd been at the team dinners Coach Gillis
hosted before, usually sitting with her mom. She always wore

sweats or her Nichols uniform. Now, she was wearing a purple dress over black leggings, and a headband to keep the hair she usually hid behind out of her face. A face that looked like it had some makeup on.

"Hi, Cleo!" Sam exclaimed, and waved at her.

"Hi, Peter," she said quietly.

"Let me help you," Sam said, taking the box of silverware out of her hands.

"Looks like you could learn a thing or two from Pete," Derek told me as we watched Cleo and Sam set up the table together.

"Huh?" I asked.

"If you were a gentleman like that, maybe things would have worked out differently with Stacey." Derek said it with such satisfaction.

"Who's Stacey?" Sam asked.

"Maz's ex," Paul piped up. It's like he loved to point out all my failures.

Sam froze. "YOU HAD A GIRLFRIEND?"

This got everyone cackling except for Cleo and Coach.

"Not just one," Paul chimed in again. "Let's see, there was Abby from Armstead, Bahar the family friend's daughter, Julie who worked at the movie theater—"

"Julie doesn't count," Quincy said, bringing a plate of cooked burgers to the table. "That lasted, what, like two weeks?"

"Two and a half," Ezra protested. "The free popcorn we scored was nice."

"Since when are all of you keeping track?" I asked.

"You didn't tell me," Sam said, his eyes still on me, the surprise in his voice replaced with hurt.

"He messed up everything with Stacey," Paul said. "And now we can't hang out at her place anymore."

"Hey, guys, maybe we shouldn't talk about this in front of the kids." Derek nodded in Sam and Cleo's direction. Sam glowered at him.

"When did we hang out at Stacey's place?" Craig asked.

"*We* didn't," Brewster grumbled. "Only seniors allowed at her party."

"Party?" Coach asked, turning around from the grill. Brewster was getting on my last, already fried, nerve.

"A birthday party," I lied. "Small group. Pizza, cake, very wholesome."

"Uh-huh." Coach placed a plate of cooked burger patties on the table before sitting down. "Well, dinner's ready. Come have a seat, everybody."

Derek and I took seats across from Cleo and Sam.

"I'm really glad to see there's a competitive spirit among you this week," Coach said, looking Brewster's way. "But don't forget, it isn't just about individual times. To win against Armstead, we're going to need to pull together as a team. I know you can win. I hope you do, too. Now, let's eat."

All the guys reached for food. I was starving and dumped piles of pasta salad onto my plate before passing the bowl to Derek.

When pasta reached Sam, he scooped a tiny bit onto his own plate. Then he started to play with his food, sliding elbow macaroni around.

"You know, the scout from Bates College is going to be at the Armstead race." Coach said it to the table, but he made eye contact with me. "Something for you seniors to keep in mind."

We all knew which senior he meant. Derek was applying early to Columbia, Quincy was a Tufts legacy kid, and Paul and Ezra didn't have the kind of race times colleges were looking for.

"We will, Coach," I said. "Vacationland! Sounds like my kind of place!" Even though I wasn't really sure if I wanted to go to Bates. Winters in Maine were supposed to be worse than ones here. It'd be great if someone from the University of Miami wanted to come to our races, then I wouldn't have to take up skiing.

"Tell me, Peter, what lessons is Maz imparting on you exactly?" Paul asked, placing a paper napkin on his lap. "Does he tell you to study hard?"

"Maz? Study hard?" Ezra laughed. "That'll be the day."

"Maz is a great student," Sam said. This got Paul laughing, too. I could see Craig suck in a smirk, but he knew better than to mess with upperclassmen. "He always helped me with home-work and got As."

Sam was right. I had been a good student. All that kind of fell to the wayside. It might have been the workload at Carter, maybe even the partying and girlfriends, but mostly I just didn't see the point in it. The game of life wasn't a long one, and if it was rigged already, why work so hard? And I wasn't failing or anything. A B at Carter was like an A at public school, or at least, that's what I explained to my parents. If I had shown up with a B before Sam went missing, I'd have gotten endless lectures about how edu-cation was so important and it was the one thing no one could take away from you, even if you had to leave your home country and start over. But after Sam went away, their focus shifted from making me great to making sure I was okay.

"Oh man, I don't know what stories he's told you, Pete," Ezra said.

"Cut it out, Ez," Derek said.

"Best friend to the rescue, per usual," Paul said.

"You're Maz's best friend?" Sam asked Derek coolly.

"I guess I have that honor, yeah," Derek said with a chuckle.

Sam didn't find it so amusing. "Who is his favorite Ghostbuster?" Sam asked, his face stone serious.

"Uh—I don't know." Derek turned to me and asked me with his eyes if this kid was for real. "I could see you relating to Bill Murray," he said.

"You mean Dr. Peter Venkman," Sam corrected him, his voice oozing condescension. "And that's not the right answer. Is it, Maz?"

"It's really not that big a deal," I said gently, trying to get Sam to relax.

"Dr. Egon Spengler is your favorite, right?" Sam insisted. I hadn't thought about the Ghostbusters in years.

"Well, sure, once upon a time," I said.

"Ghostbusters were cool," Quincy chimed in. "I always wanted a Proton Pack."

"Oh man, I still want a Proton Pack," Ezra agreed.

"I had one," Paul said, before sinking his teeth into his corn. Paul had a lot of things; our school library was named after his grandfather.

"How did Maz get a scar on his knee?" Sam asked Derek, not letting up.

"I—uh—don't know. Biking?" Derek asked, unsure. It

wasn't even that visible of a scar now that my legs were covered in hair. Sam shook his head in disapproval.

"He got it from trying to skateboard at the mall parking lot when he was nine," Sam said. "A best friend would know that stuff."

"Fair enough," Derek said, holding his hands up in defeat. "Clearly there's a lot that I missed. Though it seems like Maz tells you a lot more than he tells me." Sam opened his mouth, looking to ask Derek some more questions. I had to stop this.

"Cleo!" I said quickly. "We have got to catch up."

"We do?" Cleo asked politely.

"How are you liking school?" I glanced at Sam, who was still staring daggers at Derek.

"It's okay," Cleo said with a shrug.

"Just okay?" Coach Gillis asked, a hint of concern in his voice. "I thought you were excited about the dance on Friday?"

"*Daaaad*," Cleo said, her makeup not doing much to hide the red tinging her cheeks.

"My sister, Nilou, is going to that," I said. "It should be a fun time."

"Lou Lou is going?" Sam asked me excitedly. At least he wasn't focused on Derek any more. "Maz's sister is so funny, Cleo. You two would get along great."

"Really?" Cleo asked. "I mean, we don't really hang out in the same group."

"Trust me, you guys are both so cool. It'd be awesome to see her! Can I go?" Sam asked.

Shit.

"Uh, well, I don't think . . . um, I mean it's not—" I stammered.

"Would you like to go with me, Peter?" Cleo blurted out.

"You bet I would!" Sam held up his hand for Cleo to high five. She tapped it softly, and the red on her cheeks deepened.

"I think that's a fine idea," Coach Gillis said, mirroring Cleo's smile. "There's still a need for chaperones, Maz. You can bring Peter, stay for the dance, and drop him off at home afterward."

Double shit.

"I, um, well, I'll have to ask his mom," I lied.

"I'd be happy to get in touch with her if you give me her number," Coach offered.

"No! That's—I'll, um, see what I can do."

Sam turned to Cleo, ignoring me completely. "I'll be there, no matter what," he promised.

"That is adorable," Paul said, in between chomps of corn. "And Maz gets to babysit the widdle kiddie's playtime! I imagine it'll be a welcome break from your usual libations."

"Shut it, Paul," I said, hoping Coach didn't hear him.

"What's a libation?" Sam asked.

"A type of drink," Paul said.

"That's enough, Paul," Coach warned. Sam put it together, too, and looked away from me, his face turning pink.

"Dad, may Peter and I eat in the living room?" Cleo asked. It was a new record for when she'd had enough of us. I didn't blame her.

"Sure thing, sweetheart," Coach said.

Cleo picked up her plate and stood up, and Sam followed

her, leaving his plate behind. "Want to play Sega?" she asked as the two of them walked away from the table.

That's when Paul started to cough. He began to hack up chunks of corn. His face turned red, and he dropped the cob on his plate.

"Whoa, you okay?" Ezra asked, slapping him on his back. Coach was getting out of his seat when Paul nodded his head, still coughing, but finding it easier to breathe. He took a sip of water, cleared his throat, and wiped at his eyes.

"Went down the wrong pipe," he said.

I wasn't so sure.

❧ ❧ ❧

Sam wasn't as chatty on the drive to Cori's as he had been at dinner. He spent most of the ride staring out the window.

"Cleo seems to like you a lot," I said, unable to take the silence any longer.

"Yeah. She's really nice," Sam said. He wasn't giving me much else to work with. I put on my signal when I saw the exit for Walnut Mills. I didn't know where we were going to put Sam when Cori's parents got back the next day, but Cori and I needed to figure it out fast. "Do you like Derek better than me?"

I slowed into the turn and stopped at the traffic light before I looked at him. His expression was so solemn. I couldn't tell if I should laugh or worry. "A guy can have more than one best friend. If anyone knows that, it's you."

He accepted this answer with a nod and looked back at the road. "You should have told me you had a girlfriend."

"I didn't think that was a big deal!" The light turned green and I kept driving.

"Is it because I'm not mature enough? My dad gave me the talk, I know how stuff works."

"No! It's—I mean, Stacey broke up with me and I don't feel much like talking about it."

"Sure, you've already talked to your teammates about everything."

I turned onto Cori's street. The neighborhood was mostly quiet. There wasn't much traffic; a few kids played on a lawn in front of one of the houses. As soon as I pulled into the O'Briens' driveway, Cori marched toward us, carrying a bundled blanket. She banged on Sam's window.

"WHAT DID YOU DO TO MY DOG?"

"Hey!" I said, climbing out. "Watch the car."

Sam looked up at Cori in fear.

"What's wrong?" I asked. Cori was breathing heavily, her eyes full of fury. She shoved the bundle into my chest. Potato Chip snarled at me without uttering a growl. He looked a lot like that squirrel on the trail. "Not again."

"Again?" Cori seethed. "You knew he could do this?"

"No, not really." I'd seen this before, but I hadn't brought it up with Sam. I hadn't wanted to put two and two together.

"Get out of the car," Cori snapped at Sam. The neighbors' curtains rustled.

"We should talk about this inside," I whispered to Cori.

"I don't want him anywhere near Janet," she hissed back.

"What's going on?" Janet asked from the doorway.

Sam lowered the window by a sliver. "He's not dead," he

said softly, a hint of testiness in his voice. "Don't bury him or anything."

It wasn't an admission, but Sam wasn't playing dumb.

"Then what is the matter with him?" Cori demanded, clutching Potato Chip closer to her. "You did this to Nick, too."

"Nick?" I looked from Cori to Sam. "What happened?"

Sam squirmed in his seat, his face in a grimace.

"Nick is in the hospital." Cori's eyes did not leave Sam for a second. "What did you do to him?"

"I only wanted some more time with you two," Sam squeaked out. "To do the things I missed out on."

I swung around and gently touched Cori's forearm. She finally looked at me. Her lower lip trembled and her nose scrunched up.

"Nick was fine. You saw him! Now he's . . . You don't know how awful it was," Cori sobbed. I put my arms around her, and she curled into my chest. Potato Chip's warm, motionless body pressed against mine and I trembled. He felt like a small log of wood.

I heard a car door open and let go of Cori. Sam was running down the street. I bolted after him.

"Sam!" I yelled. He had a head start, but I was so much faster than him now. This time, I would catch him. This time, I wouldn't let him go. I caught up with him in a couple of blocks. I grabbed his shoulder. He jerked backward, his baseball cap falling to the asphalt, but he stayed on his feet. "We can work this out," I promised.

He shook me off but turned around to face me. "You've got to tell me what's going on. No more secrets."

"I can't," Sam said. He put his fists to his temples and shut his eyes. "Shut up, old man." It took me a second to realize he wasn't talking to me. He opened his eyes again, his fists lowered to his sides. "I didn't want to do it. I had to so I can stay here. Tell Cori that, okay?"

"Tell her yourself," I said, reaching for him again, but he took a step back. "The three of us together can handle anything. We can help you."

"He says you want to send me back so you can keep hanging out with your cool new friends." Who was Sam talking about? "That I'm getting in the way like I always did. He's right, isn't he? Sam the Squirt, bringing you two down when you're on the rise?"

"That's not true," I yelled. A car slowed down as it passed us. I lowered my voice again. "Let's go home."

"Home?" Sam screamed. "I don't have one anymore!"

I wanted to tell him he always had a home with me, but my throat constricted.

I couldn't talk.

I fell to my knees and started to cough.

Sam looked at me, his face crumpled, tears streaking down his cheeks. Then he started running. When I could breathe again, he was gone.

29.

CORI

MAZ BENT DOWN ON ONE KNEE and put Potato Chip's travel crate on the carpet. He reached his hands up, and I hugged my dog to my body one last time before handing him to Maz, who placed him in the crate. Maz left the door unlatched in case PC came back from . . . elsewhere.

"Should we say a few words?" Janet asked. I'd filled her in on who "Peter" really was. I could tell the whole thing creeped her out, but she was still here, helping me say TTFN to my dog.

"I don't know. I mean, Sam said he's not dead." Maz stood back up. I know the hope in his tone was meant to be some kind of comfort, but it wasn't working.

"I'm sorry I let him into the house, Potato Chip," I said, staring at the travel crate. "I'm not going to let him do this to anyone else." I crouched down, put my hand on the crate, thought about all the times PC had been there for me, then pushed him into Tiffany's closet. No one would find him. Tiffany barely visited us. When I did see her, it was when she was checked in at whatever fancy hotel she stayed at when she and Brooks were fighting. Our parents didn't know about her hotel stays. Tiffany would treat me to a fancy lunch and I'd keep her company while she complained. I hadn't heard from her in a few weeks. I supposed she and Brooks were getting along fine. "I'll look up Rob's address in the phone book, and we'll go talk to him in the morning," I said to Maz. "Pick me up at eight."

"You'll pick her up from my place," Janet said. "I'll write down the address for you."

"What?" I asked, turning toward her.

"There's no way I'm letting you stay here alone tonight."

"I don't want you involved in this," I said. "If anything happened to you or your family, I'd never forgive myself." She took my hand and pulled me toward her.

"Sam doesn't know where I live. It's just for tonight before your parents get home," Janet said.

"It might be a good idea," Maz said, rubbing his throat. "You can stay at my house, if you want?"

"No!" Janet pulled me in even closer. "I would sleep easier if Cori was with me."

I'd never seen her this stubborn before. I loved it.

"I can see that," Maz said, his eyes flicking between the two of us. Janet seemed to notice and loosened her grip on me a little. Maz blinked a few times. "I'll see you at eight."

❧ ❧ ❧

"Didn't the guy at the gas station say we were supposed to take a right back there?" Maz asked as we drove around Dover. It was like Maz's or Tiffany's neighborhoods, big houses and nice cars, but it was a more rural suburb with plenty of space and seemed like it was in the middle of nowhere.

"Keep going. I'll let you know when to turn." I watched the trees fly by as Maz picked up speed. He tapped his fingers on the steering wheel.

"Janet seems great," he said. "I'm glad she's, um—well, that she's there for you." Something in his voice made me wonder what he'd figured out about our relationship, but I was too tired to care.

"Don't," I pleaded. He listened and dropped the subject. "Remember we don't mention Sam unless Rob brings him up."

"And if he does, we don't say Sam's back. I know, Cori."

꙰ ꙰ ꙰

We sat in Rob's living room by an unlit fireplace. His house was bigger than I expected, and all his furniture looked brand-new.

He also looked much better than he did at the store. His hair was brushed back, and he didn't wear glasses anymore. He seemed in better shape than someone his age should.

"I can't believe how grown up you two are!" Rob said as he handed Maz a cup of coffee. "You sure you don't want anything to drink, Larry?"

"No thank you," I said with my practiced forced sweetness. The old nickname left me cold.

"How are things, Moe?"

"Pretty good," Maz said. "I'm applying to colleges."

"College already? Wow. That's great! My, does time fly." Rob leaned back in his chair and marveled at how grown up Maz was. "I remember when you couldn't reach the top of the comics rack, and now you're graduating high school." Rob continued to beam at Maz, evidently not giving much thought to the boy he once called *Curly*. "Larry, how are things with you?"

"Things are great!" I lied, wearing the cheery, plastered-on smile that only Maz knew was fake. "Really loving my senior year. I'm on yearbook staff," I lied again. "Our class is putting together a time capsule. Maz and I got to thinking about the newsstand, and we decided to look you up." Maz continued to smile, letting me be dishonest for the both of us. I was better at it than he was. I'd had years of practice.

"I'm glad you did," Rob said.

"You have a beautiful home," I said, trying to flatter him.

"It's not too shabby." Rob gave Maz a wink. "I loved the store, but when I had the chance to sell, well . . . they made me an offer I couldn't refuse." He said the last bit in a terrible Don Corleone accent.

"The store was the best. We had so many great times there," I said, nodding at Maz, silently begging him to back me up.

"The pinball game you had there was awesome," Maz said. My eyes almost popped out of my head, but I kept my smile in place. That was way too soon to be subtle. "What was it called again?" He rubbed his chin and faked trying to remember so hard, his eyebrows knit together. If Carter Prep had a drama club, Maz was not a part of it.

Rob pursed his lips but didn't say anything. It was a small thing, one that could be considered of little consequence to someone who wasn't paying attention.

"Uh—*Sorcerer*? Yeah, that was it! Man, was that a fun game," Maz said, shaking his head. "Did you keep it?"

"Oh gosh," Rob said, snapping back to easy, breezy conversation. "The Wallington Company said they'd take care of all the odds and ends once I signed the contract to sell the place."

"Where'd you get it?" Maz asked too quickly, almost hopping out of his seat. He must have remembered we were supposed to play this cool, because immediately after, he crossed his legs and casually looked at a hangnail on his thumb. "I mean . . . I only ask because my parents asked me what I'd want for a graduation present. I thought back to the game and all the good times we had playing it, it might be kind of cool to have one at home."

Rob leaned forward in his chair; a relaxed smile was stuck on his face.

"You can't take a pinball machine with you to college, can you?" he asked. I could see Maz struggling to come up with an answer.

"What do you get for the guy who has everything?" I joked with a shrug. "I wish I could still get those Juice Bar bubblegum candies."

"You were always a loyal customer." Rob shifted his focus to me. "Can't help you with where you can get your own pinball machine. I got mine for a steal from an estate sale."

The memory clicked into place like Tetris blocks.

"From the Davenport estate," I said, staring at Maz. His brow furrowed, but I could tell he didn't remember. The game had come from the abandoned mansion that reminded me of an Edward Gorey drawing.

"That's right," Rob said quietly. He clasped his hands together in his lap as he looked between us. He was forcing the same casual attitude we were. "But I'm sure you could find a game like that from the manufacturers. Though with all the video games I see on TV, I didn't think you kids would still be interested in pinball."

It sounded like good old Rob didn't *want* us to be interested in pinball.

"You know what they say," I said, keeping my voice peppy. "What's old is new again. So, if you have any idea how I can find that gum, it'd be much appreciated." Maz laughed a little too much at that, but Rob didn't seem to notice.

"I think they discontinued it. It's a shame—the packaging was great, even better than the gum itself! I can call my old supplier for you, but don't get your hopes up. Once something's gone, it's hard to get it back."

He paused, unclasped his hands, picked up his own cup of coffee, and took a long sip. Maz did the same, mirroring him, but his hand shook and some coffee dribbled down his chin. So much for calm questioning.

"It's great seeing you kids again," Rob said. "I know you two went through a lot."

"We did," Maz said, not having to act as if everything was fine.

"Some things are better left in the past," I said, trying to sound assuring.

"That they are," Rob agreed, enunciating each word slowly. I could have been imagining it, but there was a hint of warning in his voice. It almost sounded like a threat.

30.

"LOOK WHO I FOUND!" Dad said, leading Cori into our kitchen. Mom jumped out of her chair, rushed over to Cori, then went in for the biggest bear hug.

"Oh, Cori! It's been too long." Cori hugged her back and smiled at me. They let go of one another and took each other in. "We've missed you so much! Maziyar! Why didn't you tell us she was coming? Cori, you must stay for dinner! We just started. How are you? How are your parents? Come see Nilou—you won't even recognize her, she's such a grown-up now!"

Cori blushed, reverting back to her childhood shyness. I got that way when I saw an elementary school teacher at the grocery store. It didn't matter if you were taller or old enough to serve in the military, if you saw your second-grade teacher, you'd start acting a little childlike around them, too.

"You're so pretty now," Nilou said, her eyes wide with wonder.

"She was always pretty," Mom insisted. Cori blushed even more.

"Please, join us for dinner," Dad said.

"I'd love to, and it's so wonderful to see all of you. But I need to talk to Maziyar for a moment."

"Everything okay?" Mom asked, sensing Cori's apprehension.

"Yes!" Cori and I blurted out simultaneously, which was not particularly smooth.

"I'll be back another time when it's not a school night. If that's okay?" I didn't know if she actually meant that or was just being polite.

"You're always welcome here," Mom said. I nodded for Cori to follow me to the stairs, her backpack looking full with whatever she had found at the library. After our visit to Rob's, I had gone back to school, showing up for a few classes and practice. She rushed into the room as soon as I opened the door.

She took in my huge poster of Pamela Anderson in a red *Baywatch* swimsuit. I remembered how much Stacey hated it. My bed wasn't made, and I had a pile of clothes on the carpet that I hadn't folded and put away yet. I was expecting Cori to give me some dig about how men were gross, but instead she set her backpack on my desk and started unzipping it. "Okay, so I had some help from the librarian and I did some research on who actually owns the Davenport estate now." She pulled out a photocopy of a public record for me to read. "I don't think there was any estate sale."

"How come?"

"Because Rob owns the estate," Cori said, pointing at his name on a photocopy of the deed.

"Why would Rob own it? And why doesn't Rob live there or sell it?"

"I don't know, let's ask him," Cori said, her voice heavy with sarcasm. "I found Davenport's obituary."

She pulled out a few books along with a photocopy of a *Boston Globe* obit section. Centered in the article was a photograph of a dour-looking old white man with sunken-in cheeks. He wore a suit and tie and generally reminded me of the picture of Henry Ford in my history textbook. It looked like it was taken on his way to the crematorium. He fit the description of the old man from Sam's nightmares all right. If I saw him in my dreams, I wouldn't be able to sleep for years.

"He was only survived by one family member," Cori said. "His niece, Elizabeth Davenport."

"Why wouldn't he give her the house?" I asked.

"I figured we'd ask her tomorrow. After school work for you?"

"Practice gets out at four," I said. I couldn't skip two practices in one week or Coach would call my parents.

"Sure thing," Cori said with one hand on her hip. "Better yet, why don't we wait until the weekend? I'm sure Sam won't have caused any more damage by then."

"After school works, too," I said, and winked at Cori, who let out an exhausted laugh. "Have you eaten anything?" She shook her head. "Stay for dinner. You can't track down a dead rich guy's nieces on an empty stomach."

Cori thought about it for a moment.

"That baked ziti downstairs does smell good," Cori said, relaxing her shoulders. "Your mom's cooking is incredible. Especially that dish with the celery and beef over rice."

"Khoresht-e karafs. A classic," I said. "Not so many Persian meals these days. Since my mom started working, she doesn't have time. They take too long."

"I bet she'd be more than happy to teach you how to make it."

"I make Pop-Tarts."

31

I TOLD YOU. They don't love you anymore. They have moved on with their lives. Such is the nature of things, you dolt. Now that you have made this discovery for yourself, you must get on with what is required of you.

Do you ever get tired of your own horse crap?

I will permit you to speak to me in that way because you are ravenous, but another outburst like that and I am afraid it will not be pleasant.

Yeah, because it's been a real walk in the park since you took me away from my life.

I have given you power.

Only to help yourself! Besides, what am I going to do with it when I'm stuck inside again?

It is a temporary plane.

For you. But you're going to keep the rest of us in there, aren't you?

. . .

That's what I thought.

You know there is no avoiding the inevitable. You must return soon. Otherwise, those you have fed upon will be lost.

Better them than me.

Your friends may not see it that way. Cori seems to care about her little canine companion more than she cares about you. And Maz has a whole team of friends. They'll both be leaving for higher education soon.

It is really hard to focus when you keep yapping on. Can you save the speeches for after I eat?

You would not need to feed if you did what you are supposed to do.

I'll get to that. Thing is, I've got a date on Friday. I know you don't know anything about that. I mean, who would want to socialize with you? Gross. But I never went to a dance before and I . . . I don't want to let Cleo down. So, can it wait until then?

Bon appétit.

◗ ◗ ◗

"Icky Vickie . . ."

"Who said that?" She can't see me hiding in the branches of the tree above her. That suits me fine. "If that's you, Dennis, I'm going to tell your mom."

"Kind of late to be coming home on a school night." Vickie spins around, looking into the darkness for me.

"You're not funny, Dennis! Cut it out!"

"Who's Dennis?"

She finally looks up to the tree branch where I'm sitting. She screams.

"Man, you've sure got a pair of lungs!"

Vickie takes steps backward, moving toward her front door. She never takes her eyes off me. I jump down twenty feet and land just fine, which I can tell shocks her. The old man's power is good for something, I guess.

"This isn't real," Vickie tells herself. She's almost at her door. "You're not really here. You died, didn't you? We dressed up at the memorial and we were sad and I felt guilty—how are you here?" She trips on the steps, falling onto her butt. She crawls backward, doing her best to get away from me.

"Aww, Vickie. Doesn't look like there's anyone out here to help you. Don't you have any other friends you can call up?" I ask her. She probably doesn't even remember that this is what she said to me when I needed Cori the most. "I've got a date on Friday. Bet you can't believe that, huh? I got invited to a dance by a really nice girl who thinks I'm worth something. I don't need pity invites from the likes of you anymore."

"I . . . I shouldn't have been mean to you. When you were gone, I felt so bad." She puts her arms in front of her, as if she could fend me off.

Might as well put her out of her misery.

"Don't worry, I know how much you like Nick. You're about to join him real soon."

I loom over her, the fear in her eyes visible as my jaw begins to detach, lowering itself to the center of my chest.

I focus on her. I can feel the flames about to spark out of my pupils.

She turns to look away from me. "I'm sorry," she says in between whimpers. "I'm sorry!"

❧ ❧ ❧

What are you waiting for? Feed!
No.
I'll find another way.

32

AS SOON AS THE BELL RANG, I stopped working on my calculus test. I didn't even get to the last three questions. Grades were usually the sort of thing I'd stress about, but that seemed unimportant right now. I passed my exam to Ms. Glover.

"It's kind of a mess," I said.

"Oh, honey, that's all right." She'd never called me *honey* before, but I suppose the girl whose boyfriend was in a coma at the hospital received endearments. All I had to do these days was have my eyes well up and mention Nick, and most of my teachers let me skip class. "I imagine you've got a lot on your mind." *Lady, you don't know the half of it.* I gave her a polite nod and left her classroom. I hadn't seen Vickie all day. I guess she was taking the Nick news harder than I was, which was just another layer of guilt in the guilt lasagna that was my soul.

Janet was leaning against her locker between two of her friends.

"Hey," I said as I walked toward them. She looked at me with confusion, then glanced at both Clyde and Jeannie. "How are you?"

"We don't vote," Jeannie said, her green hair stuffed under a beanie.

"What?" I had no idea what she was talking about.

"If you're talking to us so we vote for you, you're wasting your time," Clyde said. I realized I was in uncharted territory.

"That's not why I—"

"Cori's cool," Janet said, with a small smile. "We're friends."

Clyde and Jeannie looked at each other in disbelief before they gave me a once-over.

"Yes, we are," I confirmed. Janet's smile got a little bigger. "I'm taking off, but I wanted to check in before I go."

"Catch you later guys," Janet said, pushing herself off the wall with her foot.

"Are you okay? I'm sorry I haven't been around. I've just been trying to find Sam—"

"Cori."

"Yeah?"

"We're talking together."

"Well, I feel like I'm doing most of the talking—"

"In public," Janet said, nodding in the direction of kids staring at us as we walked down the hallway.

"Is that okay? I mean, I don't want to ruin your rep or anything."

Janet let out a belly laugh. "I don't have a rep. I thought that was more of your thing."

"I don't know what's my *thing* anymore. You're one of the only real friends I have here." I wasn't ready for us to make out in public, but I wasn't going to pretend we didn't know each other anymore.

"How goes the search?" Janet asked, the knuckles of her hand brushing mine. I felt a jolt of excitement that I didn't want to ever go away.

"Maz and I have a lead, but I don't know if she's going to talk to us. Wow. I sound like a cop on a bad TV show."

"Maz and Cori has a better ring than Cagney and Lacey," Janet said.

"No way. Cagney and Lacey are infinitely cooler." I was really gay, wasn't I? "Until we find him—"

"Stay with friends, be home before dark, lock the doors, I know. I'm being vigilant," Janet assured me. "You sure you don't want me to help?"

"He's our problem," I said as we exited the building. "If he . . . froze you, I don't want to think about it."

When we got to the front of the school, Maz's car was already there, his hazard lights blinking. He got out of the car and waved at us. Janet waved back, friendlier now that she knew what he meant to me. And what she meant to me.

"Be careful," she said. "Call me so I know you're safe." I hugged her. She stiffened at first—which made sense, we were still in public—then she hugged me back.

◗ ◗ ◗

I knocked on the door of apartment 3B in a small complex in Hyde Park, hoping Elizabeth Davenport was home and would talk to us. Maz was holding a box of chocolates. His mom always told him never to go to someone's house empty-handed, but I didn't know if that applied to ambushes.

The door opened. A short and slim white woman in her sixties, wearing jeans and a button-up shirt, appeared before us, her graying red hair up in a messy bun. I had looked at enough pictures of her uncle to recognize some of her features. They had the same mouth and nose, but there was a kindness in her eyes that his severely lacked.

"Mrs. Davenport?" Maz asked.

"Ms. . . . May I help you?" She had a soft, husky voice. The pink lipstick she wore was worn down except in the corner of her lips.

"Hi! I'm Maz and this is Cori," Maz said, extending the box of chocolates. She didn't accept it. "We're sorry to bother you, but we wondered if we could ask you some questions about your late uncle."

She tensed and then began to shut the door.

"Ms. Davenport," I said, wedging my foot into the door-frame. "We need your help."

"I can't help you. I . . . I don't want to be involved," she said, her voice quavering a little.

"Trust me, we don't want to be involved either," I grunted in pain as the door continued to squeeze my sneaker.

"Our friend went missing five years ago," Maz explained for me. "He's just a kid." She didn't open the door, but I felt her stop trying to shut it. "We think it has something to do with your uncle and we don't have anyone else to ask. Please, I'm begging you. We won't take up much of your time."

Ms. Davenport froze. "My God, he really did it," she said, her voice still shaky. Then she opened the door for us and let us in.

❧ ❧ ❧

"You two like cookies?" Ms. Davenport poured out a box of Stop & Shop cookies onto a plate and placed it on the coffee table in front of us. One cookie rolled off, and Maz caught it right as it was about to fall off the table. "Sorry," she said. "I usually don't have company."

Mrs. Davenport didn't seem to have benefitted from her family's wealth. Her apartment was small; she had a new television but no stereo or CDs. The only fancy things in her living room were several thick, leather-bound books on her shelves, none of which had titles on the spines. There were a few photographs framed on the walls, some in color, but most in black and white. I assumed most were family photos, but none of them included her uncle. The color ones showed her in a nurse's uniform posing happily with other nurses and hospital staff in an office, and out at the bleachers at a Red Sox game with two gal pals. On the end was an autographed photo of Tom Selleck.

"I love cookies," Maz said, popping the one he saved from rolling on the carpet into his mouth as he sat next to me on the velvet sofa. "Thank you, Ms. Davenport."

"Call me Lizzy. Maz, right? And Cori?" We both nodded. Lizzy Davenport sat down in a pink armchair across from us.

"Thanks for the chocolates," she said, taking the lid off the box and offering them for all of us to enjoy.

"My pleasure." Maz tilted his head toward the photograph on the wall. "Did Tom Selleck really sign that?"

"He sure did," Lizzy said.

"Loved him in *Magnum, P.I.*," Maz said.

"He's the greatest," Lizzy agreed, brightening. "I normally don't go for a mustache, but he knows how to work it."

"And no one rocks a Hawaiian shirt like he does," Maz said. The two of them laughed.

"I'll have to watch reruns sometime," I lied. "Now, Ms. Davenport—"

"Lizzy," Maz corrected me, sharing a smile with her.

"Lizzy. We were hoping you could tell us about Mr. Davenport."

"I'm not sure where to start," Lizzy said, her smile suddenly gone. "I try not to think of him. You kids shouldn't be mixed up with any of this. You sure you want to know about him?"

It didn't sound like a threat, more like a plea for us to turn around.

Maz and I looked at each other. He nodded, which was all the go-ahead I needed.

"Five years ago, our friend Sam Bennett went missing. I know it sounds impossible, but we've linked his disappearance to an object that we think once belonged to your uncle."

"Was it a jukebox or game or something like that?" she asked.

"Yes! A pinball machine," Maz said, not trying to mask how thrilled he was that she knew something. "It used to be in a store in Walnut Mills called Rob's Newsstand."

"Pinball," she said, shaking her head. "He must have been desperate." She reached for a box of Virginia Slims on the coffee table, then looked up at us. "I'm trying to quit. Don't ever start smoking, okay? It's bad news." Then she slid a cigarette out, placing it between her lips. "Eight years ago, my uncle called me out of the blue. We were never close. My late mother was his sister. They had been thick as thieves until she married my father, a driving instructor, and that wasn't up to family standards I guess." She lit the cigarette, took a deep drag, turned her head, and blew the smoke away from us.

"We visited my uncle a handful of times when my grandmother was still alive. She'd be the one to invite us over. I loved to play in the garden—it was so beautiful. We'd have lunch or dinner, servants waited on us, which was so different from my regular life. We'd catch up with my grandmother, but my uncle usually didn't talk much. He never asked us how we were, what grade I was in, nothing like that. If he did talk, it was about the family business, how many employees he'd need to lay off, how hard he was working. Once my grandmother died, so did the garden. Needless to say, the invitations stopped after she passed."

She shut her eyes and squeezed the arms of her chair, her knuckles translucent as she took a deep breath, smoke billowing out of her nostrils. "Before *my* mother died, she asked me to visit her brother once in a while, so I did."

She opened her eyes but kept her gaze fixed on her lap. "He had a staff to look after his health and his house, but it was so gloomy there. Curtains always drawn, no natural light inside. He'd always get these big packages and shipments from all over the world. He'd have his people take the crates downstairs to the wine cellar. I never went down there. That was the one place my mom told me never to go." She leaned forward, dragged an ashtray toward her, and tapped the edge of her cigarette.

She lifted her eyes to us. They were pools of grayish blue, full of hurt.

"The last time I visited him, he told me he was coming to the end of his life, but he felt death was beneath him. He asked, as his only living heir, if I would help him continue."

She was silent for a moment.

"Continue what?" Maz asked.

"Living," she said. "He would grant me his estate, his entire fortune, if I helped him cheat death." She said it like it was something as simple as picking up some bananas and eggs at the grocery store.

"How was he going to do that?" Maz asked, squirming in his seat.

She tilted her head to the side, looked at us like we shouldn't have asked, then took another puff before she snubbed out the cigarette in the ashtray.

"The guy who inherited my uncle's estate could fill you in on the specifics," she said sadly. "Robert Woodson."

"Rob's in on it?" Maz asked.

"If he had that pinball machine around, then yeah. Though

I don't know if he knows how to bibbidi-bobbidi-boo the way my uncle did."

I cleared my throat, thinking I misheard her.

"Do you mean magic?" I asked, inching forward. She didn't bat an eye and my heart began to race. Sam's return opened doors I hadn't known existed. There was the possibility of so much more right under our noses.

"I don't know if I'd call it magic," Lizzy said. "But he and my mom used to go to séances before she married. They were social events for them and their friends, more of a show, something for laughs. But my uncle started to get more interested in . . . things to do with other realms."

"Sort of like Aleister Crowley?" I leaned in, eager for more details.

"Who?" Maz asked.

"He was a famous occultist," I explained.

"Oh sure, sure. We learned all about him at school," Maz said sarcastically.

"Well, I've never heard of him," Lizzy said. "But my uncle did start getting into some weird sh—stuff. My mom got some texts from him as gifts." She pointed at the bookshelf.

"Why did he use a pinball machine?" I asked, trying to keep us on topic. If the conversation lagged or moved to a tangent, Ms. Davenport might change her mind about telling us her family's dark and painful secrets. I could tell that she was facing up to something she'd long buried away. We needed to throw her a shovel.

"My uncle explained to me, when he thought I was going to take him up on his berserk offer, that he needed something that was approachable and would attract a wide range of people to get close to it. That's why he chose a game. The portal would require an annual sacrifice. If he's actually pulled this off . . . There must be others he's taken along with your friend."

"Is there a way to get the people out?" Maz asked. We'd agreed not to tell her that Sam was back unless we had to.

"If my uncle were to pass, there wouldn't be a need for any new offerings," she said. "But I have no idea how to get those that have sustained him out. There might be something in my mother's notes." She glanced again at the leather-bound books on her shelf. "I guess it's possible. If I've learned anything from my uncle, it's that anything is possible, really."

"Why didn't you try to stop him?" My question came out harsher than I meant it to. "You know about this stuff. The answer could be right there?" I stabbed my finger at her books. "Why not undo his curse?"

"This stuff *scares* me," she said defensively. "My uncle scares me. You don't know what that man was capable of. The people he was willing to hurt, the lives he was willing to crush, so long as business was booming. He had no conscience. He will get what he wants and destroy anything that gets in his way." The room was silent for a moment. We'd clearly overstayed our welcome, but Lizzy didn't tell us to leave. "I'm sorry about your friend. I really am."

"We're sorry, too," Maz said.

She locked eyes with him. Hers looked a little misty.

"What would it mean if someone did get out?" I asked. She picked up another cigarette, her hand trembling.

"That would mean that something has gone wrong."

◌ ◌ ◌

It was dusk and raining when we left Elizabeth Davenport's home. I went over the information she had given us while Maz drove. He hadn't said very much since we got into the car.

"What if we go back to Rob's and really grill him?" I asked. Maz didn't respond, he only looked at the road ahead. "She liked you. The chocolates were a nice touch."

"Sam's nightmares when we were kids," Maz finally said. "He said there was an old man reading from a book. I didn't know what he was talking about. It was Davenport."

"Summoning him, most likely."

Maz looked at me and then shook his head with disgust.

"What?" I asked.

"You say it so clinically."

"Really? You're objecting to my tone?"

"I know this is your kind of thing, but you're acting like it's happening to someone else and not to our friend."

"That's because I'm the one who isn't letting who he was to us cloud our judgment."

"You know what he said to me before he ran away? He said we wanted to send him back so we could hang out with our new friends. That he was holding us back from our great lives like he always had." Maz turned to me. "I told him that wasn't true, but I don't know if I meant that."

I felt my cheeks warm, partly because I was angry, but mostly because I felt a deep shame.

"He called me the first night I slept over at Vickie's," I admitted. "He didn't tell me what was wrong, but when he called, I wished that he would just move to Florida already." Maz didn't say anything, but I saw him nod. "What Davenport did to him isn't our fault," I said, mostly for myself.

"No. But it will be our fault if we let Sam go this time."

"We won't." I was surprised by my own confidence. I had no clue how we were going to do this.

"Every time Sam fought with Tiffany, she looked at me like I was a jerk for hanging out with him. That was the worst."

"I never understood the hold my sister had over you."

His jaw tightened as he stared straight ahead at the windy road. "How could you tell I liked her?"

"We're basically driving in Brooks's car, Maz."

"It's a great car," Maz said, hunching up his shoulders.

I snorted. "You never looked at the car in adoration the way you did her."

He braked at a traffic light and looked out his window, away from me. "You won't laugh?"

"I won't laugh," I said. "Much."

"When I was like nine, I'd daydream about Tiffany and me getting married. I thought it would be cool to be your brother for real. Then maybe you and I would be as close as you and Sam were."

"I was as close to you as I was to Sam!" He glanced at me, but the light turned green and he turned his focus back to the road. Of all the old wounds we had to heal, I never thought that was one of them. "If it felt that way, it's because he needed me more. You had people in your life who were always there for you. He didn't." Maz didn't comment. "I only had so much time left in your boys club anyway."

"What do you mean?" Maz sounded genuinely surprised.

"I was getting to the age where it wasn't usual for me to hang out with you two anymore. My dad had this whole big talk with me about it. And it wasn't just him—people would ask me 'Which one of them do you have a crush on?' Stuff like that."

"People like who?"

I looked out the windshield, catching sight of a familiar car. "Vickie."

"Who cares what Vickie said—"

"No, sorry—I mean, that's Vickie's car parked outside my house." We pulled into my driveway. Vickie was just sitting in the driver seat. Maz and I got out and headed over to her. I could see her crying behind the wheel. I started to panic. Had Nick died? I tapped on her window lightly, but she screamed anyway. She held her chest and rolled her window down.

"Don't sneak up on me like that," she gasped. When she noticed Maz, she brushed her hair out of her face and dabbed the corners of her eyes with her fingers.

"Are you okay?" Maz asked, crouching down, rain dripping down his face.

"NO!" Vickie shouted. "Would you be okay if Sam Bennett came back from the dead to taunt you?!"

❧ ❧ ❧

Maz held his letterman's jacket above Vickie's head so she wouldn't get wet walking into my house. He didn't offer *me* the jacket, but it was nice to know chivalry wasn't completely dead. It was just reserved for straight girls.

"Thanks," she sniffed.

"No worries," Maz said. His shirt was soaked, but he put his jacket back on over it anyway. He stood by my bedroom door while Vickie and I sat next to each other on my bed.

"What happened?" I asked.

"I came home last night from dance committee, which you should have *been* at by the way because Angela Nivens was being such a downer about how much the DJ we wanted would cost," Vickie said. "Anyway, I heard this voice in front of my house and at first I thought it was Monica's little brother."

"Monica Sandoval?" Maz said. "How's she doing? Does she still play soccer?"

"She's fine and she still plays soccer. She's dating Jimmy Ferrell, actually."

"Jimmy Ferrell? That guy picked his nose with his tongue up until fourth grade." Maz grimaced at the memory.

"I know! She could do so much better."

"Vickie. Focus, please," I said, pushing my hair out of my face.

"Right. Sorry. So, I think it's Dennis but when I look up and see where it's coming from, I see Sam Bennett, still twelve years old but with jacked-up hair, in a tree and smiling down at me. I know, it couldn't be, right? But I saw him!" Maz and I didn't argue with her but snuck glances at each other instead.

"Did he say anything?" I asked.

"How come you're not freaking out about this?" Vickie asked. Suddenly her wide eyes grew even wider. "You knew he was back, didn't you? Is that why you've been so weird lately?"

"That's not important right now," I said.

"I thought you were icing me out because of home-coming," Vickie said with a pout. "I could have been nominated for queen, too, you know."

"I know. You should have been," I said with a sincere smile.

She loosened her arms and dropped her hands to my comforter.

"What did Sam want?" I asked.

"He jumped like twenty feet down out of the tree and landed like a cat. Then he said something about how he was invited to go to a dance on Friday and how if I liked Nick so much, which I don't, I mean that ship has sailed and I am not anyone's second choice—"

"Vickie," I said with a sigh.

"Sam said I was going to join Nick soon. His mouth opened up, like the bottom part, lowered down and got to the size of a manhole cover, and I felt like the life was being drained out of me. It was horrible. I hated not having control or knowing what was happening. Then he was gone."

"Dance on Friday?" I muttered to myself.

"The Harvest Dance at Nilou's school," Maz said. "My coach's daughter asked him to go. He might still be planning to be there." Maz put his hand on the doorknob. "I'm going to drive around Vickie's neighborhood and look for him. You two going to be okay?"

"Yeah. Be careful," I warned him.

"You too," he said, his mouth drawn in a tight line. "Sorry he scared you, Vickie. Glad you're here." He left quickly.

"So that's why you two have been hiding out," Vickie said, staring at the door. "Is he single?"

33.

OCTOBER 2, 1992

I SLAMMED MY GYM LOCKER SHUT. It felt stupid getting ready for the race when Sam was still on the loose. I'd driven around Vickie's neighborhood looking for him for hours the other night and the night after but hadn't found a single sign that he'd been there.

I was the last one left in the locker room. I knew I had to turn out a great performance, but my head wasn't in it. I walked out of the building and toward the track. We made sure to stretch a half hour before Armstead and our small group of fans showed up. Coach Gillis and the team had their backs to me, blocking my view. The team wasn't in a huddle, and they weren't stretching. They stared at the track and field ahead of them.

"What's up every—" I said before my mouth dropped open.

A feeling of dread washed over me. I closed my eyes, taking a few breaths before I forced myself to look.

Strewn all over the track and on the field were a hundred or more members of the animal kingdom, all frozen in different scenes. Four raccoons stood up together, their paws in mid-snap and their mouths open so they looked like a barbershop quartet. Seven turkeys were stacked on top of one another in a pyramid like they were a part of a deranged Thanksgiving window display. Scattered along the lines of the track were rabbits, possums, squirrels, and chipmunks, all posed in ways that were meant to be funny but left me feeling sick. In the center of the track, where we typically stretched, seven deer stood on their hind legs, holding one another up, in their own little huddle.

There was no smell of death among the lifeless forest dwellers. Flies hovered above the catatonic critters, but they never touched them. Sam had worked up quite the appetite.

"So . . . does this mean we forfeit?" Brewster asked, breaking the silence.

"I—I don't know," Coach Gillis said, slack-jawed.

Paul bent over and retched up his lunch.

I looked back at the deer in the huddle, hooves linked together, tilted to one side and about ready to fall over. I knew this was Sam trying to get my attention. He didn't like that I was a part of a team that didn't include him. He didn't like that I was good at something, good enough to have someone from a college come check me out and maybe cause me to move away. I'd move away and he couldn't. He was angry, sure, but it occurred to me that he was doing what he'd always done when he felt Cori and I were slipping away.

"It's a test," I said aloud. I felt eyes from my teammates on me but didn't acknowledge them. "He's testing me."

"Maz?" Derek asked. I started to march back to the locker room.

"Don't touch anything," I shouted to the team. "Don't bury any of them."

"Where are you going?" I heard Quincy yell before I made it inside. I ran down the hallway, rushed to my locker, and got my car keys and wallet out of my bag. I heard footsteps behind me. I turned around to find Derek.

"Go back to the team, Derek," I said.

"Nope. I'm going with you." He planted himself in my way.

"I can't. I have to find him."

"Find who?"

"You don't want to know—if you see Sam . . ."

"Sam?"

"Peter. If you see him, stay as far away from him as you can—" I said, trying to get by him.

He stood his ground and blocked me from leaving.

"I have to GO!" I yelled.

"Why? Talk to me!"

My eyes started to well up. I turned back around and punched my locker. My knuckles throbbed. I let out a breath and sat down on the wooden bench between the locker banks. I covered my face with my hands, trying to hide away from Derek, but he was right there. I felt him sit down next to me. I took my hands away from my face and stared at the floor.

"I've never seen you this serious about anything," Derek said. "Whatever you got to do, it must be big."

If I told him everything, he wouldn't believe me.

"When I was twelve, one of my best friends was taken. Abducted. Nobody found him," I said, still looking at the floor.

Derek didn't say a word. He didn't get off the bench either.

"Peter, the kid you met, his real name's Sam. He's my second chance to make things right. He's missing and I have to find him. But he's . . . he's dangerous . . ."

"That little kid?" Derek asked with half a chuckle. When I finally made eye contact with him, his chuckle sank back in his throat. He digested what I was saying, his face shifting from confusion to worry.

"I think he's going to be at that Nichols dance tonight. If he is, I've got to talk to him. Stop him from hurting others the way he's been hurt."

I waited for Derek to get up, tell me to stop kidding around, ask me more questions.

"Guess Coach finally found his second chaperone," he said. "Do you think they'll count as community service hours?"

34.

CORI

JANET AND VICKIE HAD INSISTED ON coming with me to Maz's house. Now I sat in between them on the Shahzads' couch. Maz and I were supposed to meet up and go to the dance together, but something must have sidelined him, and I was trying not to think about what that might be. "It's so wonderful to have you all here," Mrs. Shahzad said to Vickie and me. "It feels like no time has passed since you were kids. And so nice to meet you, Janet. Have you thought about what you're going to do after graduation?" she asked all three of us.

Not as much as I should.

"I'm going to attend Bentley," Vickie said. She hadn't applied or been accepted yet, but I appreciated her confidence. "They're top-notch for studying business."

"Good for you," Mrs. Shahzad said. "Cori? What about you?"

"I've been looking at UMass Amherst," I said. I really wanted to study film at Ithaca or NYU, but those places were way out of my budget, unless Tiffany and Brooks wanted to help.

"That's a very good school. You were always so smart. Do you know what you'd like to study?"

Movie makeup and practical effects, I answered in my mind. What came out instead was: "Economics, maybe?" I felt like that would be an answer she'd be proud of.

"Really?" Mrs. S. asked. "I always thought you'd do something creative."

"I thought so, too," Janet said. "You should see some of her designs. They're phenomenal."

"I'm not surprised," Mrs. Shahzad said. "Cori was always so talented." I beamed. She hadn't seen me in years and she still understood me more than my own parents sometimes did.

"What was Cori like as a little girl?" Janet asked.

Thankfully, before Mrs. S. could regale her with stories, I heard shoes clicking down the hall and turned. Nilou twirled into the living room. She was wearing a pink dress with spaghetti straps and black ballet flats. This was the third outfit we'd seen her model so far.

"I *love* that color on you," Vickie said.

"That is beautiful, Nilou joon," Mrs. S. agreed.

"I don't know that people are going to be wearing dresses though," Nilou said. "It's not a formal or anything."

"You never need an excuse to wear a dazzling outfit," Vickie said.

"And it's your first dance," Mrs. S. assured her.

"I don't even have a date," Nilou said, rolling her eyes.

"Dates? What dates?" Mrs. S. raised her eyebrow. "You're too young for the dates."

"Dates are overrated," Janet said. "I mean, unless there's someone you want to go with but maybe can't because of societal constraints and the overpowering weight of patriarchal expectations."

"What?" Nilou asked.

"She means, go, have a fun time, and look fabulous doing it," Vickie translated.

"We're not *supposed* to have official dates, but all the girls are pairing up with boys from Carter Prep," Nilou said with a pout. She looked six years old when she did that. "Even Cleo Gillis managed to find a date and it's all Maz's fault."

"Azizam, not everything is your brother's fault."

"It is!" Nilou protested. "He brought some boy to practice with him. Cleo was there and asked him to go with her. If Maz is going to be weird and hang out with a boy my age, why doesn't he bring him here? At least let me have first dibs!"

"Nilou," I cut in, "any guy at that dance is going to be thrilled to dance with you."

"Oh, totally. I know that," she said as she fluffed her hair.

"Yeah, you do!" Vickie said, standing up and bumping hips with Nilou.

"If it's okay with your mom, maybe we can drive you to the dance?" I asked.

"It'd be so cool to walk in there with you!" Nilou squealed. "Everyone would die!"

35

"**YOU SEE HIM?**" Derek asked me. We stood in the Nichols School gym, looking around the room. Red and white balloons decorated the entrance and refreshment table. The DJ was playing music, but the kids were still assessing one another, too shy to start dancing.

"No," I said. I scanned the gym for the hundredth time, but I didn't see Sam or Cleo yet. After a while, some of the Carter boys started jumping on the edge of the dance floor like they were on a trampoline. This put some of the girls at ease. They headed to the center of the gym, dancing among themselves in small circles. You couldn't pay me to go back to middle school. Watching this, I had more sympathy for Sam. If I was stuck being twelve forever, I might cause some damage, too.

In a ripple, all the boys and girls that weren't dancing turned their heads toward the gym entrance. I followed their lead. Nilou stood there wearing a pink dress, looking very pretty, but I knew everyone was staring at the trio of high school hotties she walked in with. I didn't know if it was the lighting, but Vickie was looking even better than usual. Nilou grinned, her head held high. I felt a tiny pang of jealousy. I knew my sister wouldn't be that proud walking in here with me.

Cori didn't seem to notice the eyes on her. I suppose she was used to being stared at. Even in the most casual clothes, she was an absolute knockout. When they all walked over to us, I could feel all the awkward boys in different phases of puberty rooting for Derek and me.

"See anything interesting yet?" Cori asked.

"No."

Nilou waved to a few of her friends.

I smiled at my sister. "Wow, Nilou! You look beautiful! Maybe you can save me a dance?" Nilou gave me a frightened glance. "Or not."

"Please don't, like, come around me and my friends, okay?" She seemed a little apologetic. "If boys see you crowding me, none of them are going to ask me to dance."

"Yeah, Maz," Vickie teased. "You'll totally ruin her vibe."

"I will stay away," I said, crossing my heart. "You have a ride home?"

Nilou nodded, waved to us, then flitted off to find her friends. The lights dimmed; more kids descended upon the dance floor.

"You were right," Cori said, a small smile on her face as she watched Nilou laugh with her friends. "She's a cool girl."

"Takes one to know one," I said.

"I don't feel so cool right now. I feel like a nervous wreck."

I put an arm around her shoulder. She gave me a small hug back. I guess it didn't feel so strange for Cori to be close to me anymore.

There was a group of middle school girls standing by the refreshment table. Cleo Gillis was with them. Her hair was up and out of her face, and her dress was white and frilly. It didn't fit her quite right, but she looked adorable. Her eyes kept straying to the balloon arch at the entrance. She was waiting for Sam. I broke out in a cold sweat.

"Cleo's here," I said to Cori, tilting my chin in the girl's direction. All of us stiffened, screening for Sam like we were in a high stakes game of *Where's Waldo?*

The music got louder. "Motownphilly" started and kids whooped and hollered.

"I love this song," Vickie said, clapping her hands. "Are we allowed to dance or does that interfere with the heroics? I'm Vickie, by the way," she said, introducing herself to Derek.

"I'm Derek. Nice to meet you."

Then the record screeched to a halt. All the lights in the gym went out. The kids screamed with excitement; a few of the teachers murmured about a generator. Before anyone panicked, the lights came back on, still dim, but bright enough you could see people's faces. I noticed a brushed-back tuft of blond hair beside the DJ. I saw Sam whisper something to him, and the DJ shrugged.

"All right, we've got a request for an oldie but a goodie," the DJ announced. "This one goes out to Cleo from Peter."

Sam, still wearing the Bart Simpson sweatshirt I got him, strutted over to Cleo as "If This Is It" by Huey Lewis and the

News started to play. Cori moved to rush toward him, but I put a hand on her arm to stop her.

"Let him have this," I said.

She stilled, and we both watched Sam lead Cleo by her hand to the center of the dance floor.

Sam was a little shorter than Cleo, but she didn't seem to mind as she wrapped her arms around his shoulders, the two of them swaying together. He hesitated, unsure where to put his hands at first, but he ended up resting them on her upper back. A bunch of kids studied them, then paired off to do the same.

"Is it safe for him to be out there?" Vickie asked me. I didn't know, but I didn't think he'd hurt Cleo. The other kids that awkwardly clung to one another's shoulders and moved out of sync had no idea who they were sharing a dance floor with. Sam let go of Cleo so he could twirl her. She giggled as she spun around, inspiring the other boys to do the same to their dance partners. Sam was enjoying himself, not at all self-conscious. When it got to his favorite part of the song, he broke out into a fake guitar solo. He lip-synched the lyrics to Cleo and twirled her again.

"Looks like the only thing dangerous about him are his dance moves," Derek said, patting me on the back. I wanted him to be right.

The song came to an end. Sam kissed Cleo's hand and she blushed. He whispered something to her. Cleo grinned, Sam excused himself, and a crowd of squealing girls huddled around Cleo to get the info on the mysterious gentleman in the dirty sweatshirt.

"Hey, guys," Sam said, approaching us. He looked paler than usual, the dark circles under his eyes more pronounced.

"I never went to a dance. Wanted to see what all the fuss was about." All the other kids here would go on to have many more dances full of ill-fitting outfits, awkward slow jams, and lousy punch. They didn't know how good they had it.

"You had some great moves out there," Derek said, holding up his hand for Sam to slap. Sam obliged him.

"Thanks. I'm sorry I was kind of a jerk at the dinner. It wasn't cool. I, um—I haven't been myself lately."

"We all have bad days," Derek said, unaware of what one of Sam's bad days looked like. Vickie and Janet, who knew better, planted themselves on either side of Cori, standing their ground.

"I'm also sorry about the race today," Sam said, this time to me.

"How did you know the race got canceled?" Derek asked.

"Word gets around fast," Sam said, still focused on me, his voice weak and lower lip trembling. "I hope it didn't mess up your future plans. Really. With the Bates coach and—"

"You shouldn't have—" I stopped myself. "I'm always going to be your friend, Sam. No matter where I go or what I do."

Sam sucked in his lower lip and looked down at his muddy sneakers. He sighed, composed himself, then looked up and spoke to Derek, Vickie, and Janet.

"Do you think I could talk to Maz and Cori alone for a minute?" Sam asked.

I nodded, letting the others know we were okay.

"You aren't going to . . . you know?" Vickie asked him, opening her mouth in a too-wide yawn. Sam shook his head. "Just checking! I'm going to go talk to the DJ, see what his rates are. Come on, Janet."

Janet stayed behind a moment to whisper something into

Cori's ear, then followed Vickie and Derek to the dance floor. It was just the three of us.

"I have to go back in, don't I?" Sam asked.

"No," I argued. "There's . . . there's got to be a way to keep you here. You and I can live on a ranch—or in some cabin in the woods, so you can get all the animals you need."

Sam shook his head. "It wouldn't be enough." He turned to Cori. "Tell him."

She didn't respond.

"You'll be glad to be rid of me," Sam said.

"There's no way we'll ever be rid of you, Sam," Cori said as she stared straight at him. "No way we'll ever be glad about it, either."

Sam gave us a hint of a smile. "There's a few stops I have to make," he said. "Before I have to go."

"We'll take you wherever you want," Cori promised.

Sam nodded, then turned his head to look at all the kids "his age" having a great time on the floor. "Is it okay if I dance a little more before we have to go?"

I looked at Cori, wondering if she'd let him. The tears building up in her eyes told me all I needed to know.

"Have fun," Cori said.

Sam rushed back into the fray, bumping into Nilou. She turned to look at him, and I thought for sure she would freak out. Instead, he apologized to her. She brushed past him, not realizing who she'd stumbled into.

36.

CORI

IT WAS PITCH-BLACK when the dance let out. I had to use my high beams and drive slowly. Derek was following us in his car, Janet and Vickie riding along with him. Maz sat in the passenger seat while Sam sat in the back directing me where to go. We didn't turn the radio on or talk much; the finality of what we were about to do, whatever it was, was sinking in.

"Turn right here," Sam said. As soon as I did, I knew where he was taking us. The old Victorian mansion sat up on a hill at the end of the street, seeming to turn its nose up at the rest of the houses in the neighborhood.

"The Davenport estate," I said.

"Home sweet home," Sam said sourly.

I parked and Sam climbed out of the car, waiting for the two of us to follow.

Maz stared up at the foreboding pyramidal turret at the top of the abandoned house. "We really have to go in there?"

"It's fine," Sam said casually. "We're invited. Now, come on, don't be chickenshit. We've got to get a move on."

The two of us got out of the car. Taking our cue, Derek, Janet, and Vickie exited Derek's, staring up at the house as they joined us. Sam began to walk up the long brick path, past the wrought iron fence, and to the long double front doors.

"You're kind of loving this, aren't you?" Maz asked me.

I kind of was.

"Does he live here?" Derek asked.

I guess the girls hadn't briefed Derek on all of the Sam-related details on their ride over.

"Let's go," I said, leading the way. When we caught up to Sam, he'd already opened the door.

"How'd you get in?" I asked, entering the dark house.

"A key!" Sam said in his Pee-wee Herman voice. "Duh!" He grinned at us, then tapped his temple with his finger. "The old man told me where to find it."

"Do you mean Davenport?" I asked. "He talks to you?"

"Does he ever! He sure likes the sound of his own stupid voice." Sam pushed his finger harder against his head for a moment. "Speaking of the windbag, you think we could have some light in here?"

The bulbs of a chandelier hanging high above us flashed on, showcasing a grand bifurcated staircase flanked with banisters that featured ornate carvings of birds. The rest of the room was filled with covered furniture, including a sheet loosely draped over a grand piano that was surely out of tune.

"How did he do that?" Derek asked Maz. "That must be one

hell of a powerful Clapper." Derek clapped his hands to try and turn off the lights, but nothing happened.

"Okay, let's find the dumb thing," Sam said, as he turned to the right and walked into another room, obviously familiar with the cavernous manor.

I took a step forward, and Maz gave me a flat tire.

"Ow," I said, my shoe almost slipping off my heel.

"Sorry." I could feel his breath on my hair.

"Little space?"

"Sure, sure." He took half a step back, but as soon as I moved, I could feel him right behind me again.

"This place would be amazing for the Halloween dance," Vickie said, traipsing up the grand staircase, not at all scared by the dreary house. "Do you think the owner would rent it out for a few hours? Wow, if I landed this place, Angela would have a fit!"

"Vickie! Stay with the group," I hissed.

She turned around on the stairs and saw the four of us bunched up together. "Oh. Right," she said, slowly descending the stairs to join us, resting her hand on the banister like she was royalty. "But you're missing out on the potential of this place, Cori. This is the perfect type of staircase for formal dress photos."

"You have to respect her devotion to the dance committee," Janet mumbled.

We followed Sam into a study, where a large desk stood in the center, covered like the rest of the furniture. The bookshelves lining the walls proudly displayed hundreds of leather-bound tomes, like the ones in Lizzy's apartment. Hanging above a fireplace behind the desk was an oil painting of Mr. Davenport. He was younger than the photo we'd seen in his obituary; here he had blond hair and more weight on his bones. But the same unforgettable cold eyes looked out at us, a piercing gray gaze that somehow said, *You are small. You are weak. How dare you come here.*

"Cheerful-looking fellow," Derek said. "One of Paul's relatives?"

Maz let out a noise that I think was meant to be a laugh, but it sounded like a whimper.

Sam walked casually to the desk, lifted up the cloth tarp, opened a drawer, and pulled out a candle and a box of matches. He didn't bother closing the drawer or covering the desk again. He lit the candle. The flame underneath his chin caused shadows to dance across his face, as though he needed any more help being scary.

"Muahahaha," he said, breaking out in actual giggles.

Vickie flinched.

"Too soon?" Sam asked. Vickie nodded. "Sorry." Sam held the candle away from his face. He crouched into the large fireplace, pressed against the brick wall with one hand. "Someone want to help me push?"

I rushed over, bent down, and pushed along with Sam. The brick facade creaked open, and behind it was a narrow staircase.

"A secret passageway!" I shrieked in glee. I mean, it was so cliché, but I'd never actually *seen* one in real life!

"I'm glad one of us is having a good time," Maz said. "I think I'll stay up here."

"Yeah, same for me," Derek said, looking around the study. He walked toward the bookshelves, examining the spines. "This guy, um"—he nodded up at the painting of Davenport—"he's not going to mind we're in here?"

"He hates it," Sam said. "Make yourself at home! Take whatever you like, that'll really get his goat." The lights in the study flashed, then went out completely, shrouding all of us in darkness. I heard Maz yelp. When the lights came back on, he was clutching Vickie's arm.

"Must have been a faulty fuse," Derek said.

"No. He's trying to show who is boss, like he's Tony Danza or something," Sam said, pointing at his temple. He climbed into the passageway. "Watch your step."

I was the only one who moved to follow him, but as I did, Janet grabbed my hand. "Are you sure it's safe to go down there?" she asked.

"No idea," I said, leaning in close to her ear. "But I'm trying to be a bit braver these days."

"I—" Janet looked behind me.

"It's okay," I said, knowing she wasn't coming with me. "You're already the bravest person I know." I kissed her cheek, then followed Sam.

I put my hand against the cool stone wall to keep my balance on the curved stairs, following the light of Sam's candle. We went slowly, and I felt the occasional cobweb brush against my skin as we descended into the bowels of the Davenport mansion.

"Yeah, yeah, I know you don't want anyone but me down here," Sam muttered. "Sorry, Cori. Davenport's talking up a storm. He asks that you not touch anything or you'll regret being born, blah, blah, blah."

At the bottom of the stairs, Sam lit a torch strapped to the wall by a sconce. He pulled it off the wall and handed me the candle. We kept going. The flames created shadows on the stone walls, and an occasional bug skittered away from us. I thought about what might be waiting for us. Talismans? Secret scrolls? Skulls? Crystals? Horrible human experiments gone wrong?

As we moved deeper into the basement, the walls were lined with . . . bottles. Wine bottles. Tons of them, sitting in racks.

"Are they potions?" I asked.

"No," Sam said. "It's really a bunch of wine. I don't know why people like it so much."

We reached the back wall, and Sam shone his light on the lock of a medium-size safe. "Can you hold this up so I can see the numbers?" I took the torch, raising both it and the candle above the lock so Sam could see. He turned to the correct numbers, the lock clicked, and he twisted the handle of the safe and opened it. He reached in, felt around, then pulled out a red leather book.

"Okay, we can go now."

"That's it?" I asked, and realized my voice sounded petulant. "I mean, don't you need something else? Like, I don't know—a mystical candle or skull or something?"

"Trust me, the book does plenty," Sam said in a huff. "You've seen too many movies." I held the light away from me so he couldn't see me blush. "Our next stop isn't something I want to put you through. Or them." I gave Sam the candle, and he pointed it toward the ceiling. "Might be a good time to tell your friends to head home."

❧ ❧ ❧

All of us stood by Derek's car in the dark. The home that had once belonged to a lonely and twisted man seemed to watch us as the lights inside continued to flicker. When Sam turned his back on the estate, the lights inside went out.

"How . . ." Derek asked.

"We'll explain on the ride home. Or try to," Janet said. Derek had offered to drive them to Vickie's. I sort of wish I could have been a fly on the wall to see the two of them hang out. One on one. They were absolutely going to talk about me.

Sam held his hand out to Derek. "Thanks for looking out for Maz," he said.

"That's what friends do, right?" Derek joked, glancing at Maz. Derek gave him a low five. "Hope to see you around."

"Yeah. Hope so," Sam said. Then he faced Vickie. "I, um—I'm really sorry about trying to suck your life essence out of you."

"Wait, what?" Derek asked.

"You should be! You scared the crap out of me." Then she softened. "But I'm sorry, too. I was kind of a jerk to you when we were younger."

"Kind of," Sam said. "People change, though." Then Sam took a step toward Janet. She didn't back away. "I wish we had more time together. Cori thinks you're the coolest so that makes you the coolest in my book."

"Hey!" Vickie objected.

"Ladies, it's possible to have more than one best friend," Sam said. Then he walked to my car, sat in the back seat, and waited for me and Maz to say our goodbyes.

"Such an intense kid," Derek said.

"Are you two going to be all right?" Janet asked.

Maz and I looked at each other, not sure of what the night was going to bring.

❧ ❧ ❧

Sam pushed the doorbell. The déjà vu was so strong, I half expected him to say *trick or treat*.

It didn't take long for Rob to greet us.

"Larry, Moe—" Rob cut off when he looked down to find Sam staring up at him.

"Nyuk, nyuk, nyuk," Sam said, channeling Curly, but in an unsettlingly calm tone of voice.

Rob's eyes widened for about two seconds. I was waiting for the old man to scream, pass out, or do a double take and ask us what the hell kind of prank this was. Instead, he let out a long, heavy, pent-up sigh.

"I figured this day was coming." Rob opened the door a little wider and let us in. "Let's hash it out."

Maz's brow furrowed with confusion and worry. I shrugged and followed Sam into Rob's house.

"May I get you all anything?" Rob asked, looking over his shoulder at us. "I've got some candy, even. No Melody Pops though."

"The only thing we want from you are answers," I said.

"I know. Still, I'd feel strange not offering." Rob led us to his living room. The room was lit by a lamp and the fireplace, whose amber flames made shadows fly around. Rob extended his hands, motioning for us to sit. All of us remained standing. Our hospitable host took a seat on his couch, spread his legs, and rested his elbow on the armrest. A glass of whiskey was already on the coffee table in front of him. He picked it up and took a small sip. "You look good, son," Rob said to a stone-faced Sam. "These two never gave up on you. I'd kill to have friends like that. It's tough, when you get older, finding people that'll go to bat for you."

"Shame I can't find that out for myself," Sam said, his voice still completely neutral. "I'm not getting any older."

"No, I suppose you aren't. Huh." Rob tilted his head, his mouth open for a moment as he marveled at Sam's appearance. "I never understood how that damn machine worked. Not fully."

"But you knew what it was doing?" Maz asked. Rob took another, longer sip. He cradled the glass in his hands while he peered up at us.

"The old man didn't give me the details about how it worked, only what he needed it for. I humored him, told the kook what he wanted to hear so he'd sign everything over to me," Rob said without a hint of remorse. "I didn't think it would work, but when it did, well, I left it in the store."

"How *could* you?" Maz's voice was dripping with bitter anger.

I lunged forward, my palm open, cocked back to slap Rob, but Sam put his arm in front of me.

Rob paused a minute, chewing his lip, considering what he was about to say. "Let me tell you kids a little something about the American Dream," Rob started, leaning back in his seat. "A man figures if he works hard, he can be in charge of his own destiny. He can make a decent living, pay his taxes when they're due, and maybe, if he's lucky, he can support a family of his own. Well, I'm sad to say, that's not always the case. Your first business might not cut it, you rack up some debts, and the economy might go down the crapper overnight. The seventies were not a good time for your old pal Rob."

"You're not our pal," I spat.

"Fair enough." Rob nodded. "The store was never very lucrative. I was paying off my debts but not fast enough. I never had that house with the picket fence. I had a cramped apartment with a pullout sofa bed. I never had much luck. Until I saw an ad in the paper. 'Wanted: small business owners looking to expand,'" Rob said with a gleam in his eye. "I went to a seminar at the Holiday Inn. There were maybe twenty or so of us there. We all filled out a survey and got a slide-show presentation on advertising and franchise opportunities. After a few days, I get a call from the fellows running the seminar. They liked how I answered the survey. They asked if I'd be willing to interview for a once-in-a-lifetime opportunity. After a few rounds, I get to meet old man Davenport. I thought he was off his rocker, but when I heard everything he was offering me—his house, his company, his holdings—in return for putting a game in my store, well, how could I pass that up?"

If he was trying to get us to sympathize with him, it wasn't working. Rob took a huge gulp of his whiskey, emptying the glass before setting it down again.

"The pinball machine was my idea. He thought it was a little too on the nose, the *Sorcerer* bit. I told him pinball had been a real crowd-pleaser for decades and it'd outlast any of the newer stuff."

"Until you moved it," Sam said. Rob's smile faltered as he took in the twelve-year-old in front of him.

"The Wallington Company buyout last year was a part of the luck Davenport said the machine would bring. I already did what the old man wanted by keeping his house empty. What difference did it make where the machine went, so long as people kept playing it?"

"Only nobody's been playing it," Sam said. "He doesn't care for that at all, Rob."

Rob squinted at Sam, a pathetic scoff leaving his mouth.

"Too bad the old man is gone. Not much he can do about it," Rob said.

"You sure about that?" Sam asked, a grin spreading on his face along with an icy glare. He held up the book and showed it to Rob. "He says it's time to collect."

Rob stood up slowly.

"That's rich. Listen, kid, I'm glad you got out and no hard feelings. It wasn't anything personal. I thought the game would pick Moe, to be honest, but I guess it figured Moe would have more people looking for him."

"How could you do that?" Maz asked, his voice pitchy and loud. "We trusted you! And what, we were just sacrificial lambs to you?"

"No," Rob said, all the mirth from his eyes gone. "You were also customers."

"You're a monster," Maz said. Rob flinched at this. "I knew those eyes on the game were watching me!"

I could see Maz spiraling. All the memories that he'd been told weren't true, that he'd long buried, were being validated. He looked like he was about to explode.

"I'm not proud of it," Rob said. "I don't expect you kids to understand, but I had to get what I needed. What I was owed."

Sam inched closer to Rob.

"I think our happy reunion has come to an end," Rob said. "Time for you to head on home." He took one step forward and then froze. His foot hovered an inch off the floor, but he didn't put it down. It took me a second to realize that he couldn't. His face twisted with confusion.

Sam had his eyes set on Rob.

"What's this?" Rob asked.

"Like I said, he's ready for you."

Rob licked his lips, then looked past Sam at Maz.

"Would you get a load of Curly?" Rob said with a tremor in his voice, still unable to will his body to move. "Thinks he's a tough guy."

"I am a tough guy," Sam said cheerfully.

A blinding beam of orange light shot out of Sam's eyes and surrounded Rob, who looked like he was stuck in a wind tunnel, his eyelids pushed back. Rob choked, struggling to get air in his lungs, as a light blue mist accumulated in his open mouth.

"Sam! Don't!" I heard Maz yell.

I couldn't move or speak. But even if I could have stopped Sam, I wasn't sure I wanted to.

Rob convulsed in the beam of light and levitated off of the floor, his legs and arms stuck straight out, energy pulsing through him. Our candy man made noises—squeals and coughs and gags—that I would never be able to forget for the rest of my life.

There was an excruciating cracking that sounded like bones breaking. I tore my eyes away from Rob floating in the air to look at Sam. The noise came from his mandible. The skin around his mouth stretched until his flesh became taut, ready to snap as his lower jaw, slowly and grotesquely, lowered. The veins near Sam's temples were pronounced, turning from purple to blue, as his jaw continued to descend down to his knees. His mouth emitted a wall of screams and screeches that didn't belong to him. Some sounded human, some animal, some sounded not of this earth. All of them grew louder and louder as his mouth widened and expanded to the size of a Hula-Hoop.

The light from Sam's eyes grew brighter. The blue mist from Rob's mouth traveled through the air, floating, until it almost reached Sam.

"Stop," Rob choked out. "I'll go."

The orange light blinked out in an instant. The screams that belonged to others went silent. Rob landed on the floor with a painful thud.

"HOLY SHIT!" Maz yelled, hands over his ears, his eyes huge and watery.

Sam's mouth retracted and went back to normal in a span of a second. He blinked. Then he turned to me.

"Are you scared?" he asked with a vicious little smile. It was the first time that I felt he wanted us to be terrified of him.

"For you, not of you," I answered.

Sam's smile evaporated as he stared down at a shivering Rob. "Don't worry, Cori," Sam said, a note of sadness in his voice. "You won't have to be for much longer."

Maz was the one who went over to Rob, helping the gasping man up but also keeping an arm on him so he couldn't run. Not that any of us could have run from Sam.

"I'm so sorry, Sam," I said, looking at our friend who had turned into some kind of a vampiric, soul-stealing Renfield sent to do the bidding of a twisted monster of a man.

"I need my pills," Rob said, leaning on Maz and looking at Sam for permission.

"Fine, but hurry." Sam adjusted his jaw with his fingers, making sure it was back where it was supposed to be. "It's time to play."

37.

MAZ

I WATCHED ROB THE ENTIRE RIDE to Tiffany's house. He was sweating, his hair was thinner with new patches of white, and the wrinkles around his eyes were deeper. It seemed the closer we got to our destination, the more his age started to catch up with him.

"You lied to us about where the machine was," Cori seethed at Sam.

"I said it was in a basement I hadn't been in before," Sam replied.

"It was in my sister's house this whole time!" Cori sped down the empty street. Sam looked up at the ceiling of the car and started to whistle nonchalantly. "I can't believe you!"

"Yeah well, I am pretty unbelievable." Sam still clutched the red leather book, which lay on his lap. When Cori parked, I could see beautifully sculpted bushes lining a brick pathway to a gigantic modern home.

"Wow," I said, intimidated by how well Brooks had done

for himself. Then again, he'd had a lot of help. The house was smaller than Davenport's, but everything looked brand-new.

"Rob's going to need some help getting inside," Sam said to me from over his shoulder.

"I knew you cared," Rob said with a groan. He didn't look right. Whatever Sam had done to him had weakened him. I got out of the car and opened Rob's door. He put his arm around my shoulder as I helped him up. We followed Sam and Cori down the pathway to the house. I gulped when Cori rang the doorbell. A giant gonglike chime sounded.

"They're not going to answer," Sam said sheepishly.

"You didn't," Cori said, slowly turning to him. "Are you kidding me?!"

I realized that Sam must have petrified them.

"They're going to be okay," Sam promised. "I think. Pretty sure."

"You are such—ugh—I can't." Cori dug into a potted plant and pulled out a spare key. I could feel Rob's labored breathing on my neck. I shifted, slightly, to change his angle. When Cori unlocked the door and an alarm system began to beep, she rushed inside to punch in the code. There was a stale and musty odor to the house, not awful or truly unpleasant, but it let me know that no one had opened a window for a while. Cori turned on a light, and I stared at our surroundings in disbelief.

"I didn't know the Wallingtons were, like, *this* wealthy," I whispered. Brooks and Tiffany's home looked like something out of one of my mom's issues of *Architectural Digest*.

"Don't worry," Cori said over her shoulder as she charged up one of the curved staircases. "Tiffany did."

I walked under the second giant chandelier of the night with Rob by my side. I guess nothing says money like a fancy chandelier, but how do they get up there to change the bulbs?

"I can stand on my own, Moe," Rob said, his breathing more even.

"You sure?" I asked as he let go of my shoulder.

"Yeah. I guess it's time to pay the piper." He wiped his mouth with the back of his hand, some color returned to his face. "The machine's close. Can't you feel it?" he asked.

I shook my head.

"That's good. I'm glad it didn't get its hooks into you."

"Are you? You seemed fine with it getting its *hooks* into people," I replied.

Rob looked like an older version of how I remembered him. He wasn't wearing his glasses, so he squinted a lot. "I made a deal with Davenport," he said. "But I didn't think it was real. When the machine came to the store, well it made me . . . it made me stronger. Made me forget about what it was there to do. It spoke to me sometimes. When it did, its voice sounded like my first love, Rose. She told me when to leave a customer alone, when to leave the door unlocked, who might be a good fit."

We heard Cori scream. Rob grabbed hold of my wrist and held it tightly. Sam flipped through the tattered and worn pages of the red book, not even batting an eye. Cori emerged, glaring at Sam from the landing high above us.

"She looks terrified!" Cori said, slamming her hand against the staircase banister.

"She'll be fine! Jeez," Sam said as he looked over a page. "Old man says this is it." He handed the open book to Rob, who held it against his chest.

Cori stomped down the stairs. When she reached Sam, I thought she might punch him.

"You couldn't have placed them in a nicer position?! Brooks was in the middle of shaving," Cori said, throwing her hands up in the air.

"I was starving!" Sam said.

"Moe, can you hold this a minute?" Rob asked me, offering me the book as Cori and Sam continued to bicker.

I looked at him with skepticism.

He let out an exhausted sigh. "I know you shouldn't trust me. But I got nowhere to run. I'm sorry I got you kids into this. I'm trying to make it right."

I took the book from him, making sure not to lose the page Sam had opened to. It was covered in a bunch of symbols, but I didn't recognize the language. Rob reached into his pocket and pulled out a bottle. He poured two pills into his hand and popped them both into his mouth like they were breath mints. After he swallowed, he took a deep breath and waved me over.

"I'll take it back now," Rob said, and I passed the tome over to him. "Don't think too badly of me, Moe. If you could, remember the good times when I'm gone. I know that's a lot to ask, but I'd appreciate it."

"Uh, guys," I said to Cori and Sam. But they just kept arguing.

"You must have *loved* getting back at her like this," Cori said, towering over Sam.

"I feel bad about it! Sort of," Sam countered.

"Hey!" I yelled, and both of them turned to look at me. "What's the plan?"

Sam tilted his head in Rob's direction. "He needs to hold up his end of the bargain. Come on. Let's get started." He walked ahead of us, leading Cori through her sister's house. Rob straightened his posture and regained his balance. He followed Sam without needing any assistance, his head hung, ready for his fate.

"What's happening?" I asked Cori.

"We're going to stop the machine, I guess," she said.

"Yeah, but how?"

"You think I know, Maz?" Cori snapped. "But my sister, my brother-in-law, my dog, and my ex are *stuck*. And they need help. So, let's see how this goes."

Brooks had made the basement into his own rec room. There was a small bar, a Ping-Pong table, a dart board on the wall, and large framed vintage travel posters of landscapes in Hawaii, Italy, and Switzerland. The *Sorcerer* machine stood in the corner of the room. Sam and Rob beelined to it.

"That's it?" Cori asked. I knew what she meant. It looked so . . . dinky and nowhere near as large or menacing as I remembered it. It was unplugged, and there was a deep crack in the glass of the display board. It'd seen better days. Was it always so small?

"Let's get this show on the road," Sam said, snapping his fingers.

The machine hummed, and a burst of bright amber light filled the room with a preternatural glow. Brooks's man den looked like it was about to be abducted by aliens. The robotic "FEEL MY POWER!" filled the room, and with it the ground beneath us trembled and the posters on the walls rattled as they shook.

"Start reading," Sam commanded Rob, his arms crossed over his chest. Then he turned to us. "You two better stay back a little. This might get messy."

I grabbed Cori's hand. She squeezed mine back, and we both retreated toward the bar. Rob began to read. Whatever language it was, I didn't recognize it. I took Latin, which was a dead language, but this seemed like a dead-and-buried-in-the-ground language.

The game's red eyes lit up, focusing on Rob. I remembered the first time I saw them move, watching us when we were kids, figuring out which of us would make the best prey. The digitized music grew louder and louder, and then the same blue mist that had left Rob's mouth at his home began to pour from the painted dragon's nostrils. Rob continued to read, the words coming faster and faster. The mist swirled like a tornado until it grew into a sphere surrounding the game. The wall behind the machine was gone. At first, I thought it had just turned black, but then I saw star clusters and planets, ones that didn't look like they belonged in the solar system we studied in school, quickly fly by in the darkest nothingness, racing at speeds I had never seen. This was a portal.

"He's coming," Sam stonily yelled over the music.

The blue mist drifted over Rob's head as he chanted, the sweat on his forehead glistening in the light. Eventually the mist flew into Rob's nostrils. Rob dropped the book and screamed as the mist vanished inside him. His body shook like he was being electrocuted. Then he collapsed facedown on the floor. Cori squeezed my hand so tight I thought she might crush my bones.

"Should we help him?" I asked her. "Is he dead?"

"Look," Cori said, tugging my hand, pulling me closer to her. "He's moving."

Rob put both his palms against the floor and slowly pushed himself up.

When he stood, he looked the same but also like a completely different person. His posture was perfect, his head held high, his chin proudly jutting out, as he slowly turned around to observe us. His eyes were cold.

"Are you the two who kept Sam from performing his duties?" Rob's voice wasn't Rob's at all. It was deeper, with a more refined, mid-Atlantic accent.

"Are you Mr. Davenport?" Cori asked.

"It is not polite to answer a question with another question," Rob said as he picked some lint off his sleeve. "However, because I am in such a delighted mood: yes. I am William Davenport."

Sam walked over to us and stood next to Cori. Davenport gave him a tiny smirk.

"Okay, it worked. Now can I say goodbye to my friends?" Sam asked.

"I'm not entirely sure I think it is wise for them to leave, now that they know about this transference." Davenport's eyes narrowed suspiciously as he looked at Cori. "Unless they are willing to listen to my proposal."

Sam stood in front of Cori, blocking her from Davenport.

"This body, as grateful as I am for Mr. Woodson's participation, won't last forever. He saw the merit in being well off for a time. I wonder if either of you would feel the same?"

Davenport then took one long stride toward me. I felt my entire body prickle. "You'd have your university tuition paid for, a high-up company position in my empire, the means to do all the things you have cared to do. Then, when the agreed-upon time came, well, it doesn't seem like such a bad deal, does it?"

"We want nothing to do with you, you prick," I said.

Davenport pursed his lips and raised an eyebrow. He turned around, clasped his hands behind his back, then walked closer to the machine.

"That puts us in quite an unpleasant predicament," he said, pivoting to face us. "I can't have you tell anyone about this. Though frankly, who would believe you?"

"Your niece would," Cori said.

Davenport let out a guffaw. "She's afraid of her own shadow. She won't help you, especially if you are not here anymore."

"That's not happening!" Sam stretched out his arms, trying to shield us.

"Why, I would be doing you a favor for your good work, Sam. You'd have all the time in the world with your friends. Isn't that what you wanted? Infinite playtime?"

Sam's shoulders slumped. My stomach twisted. We all knew how much he wanted that, and maybe Davenport's offer didn't sound so bad to him. Cori and I might be sitting ducks down here. After a moment, Sam puffed out his chest, snapped his shoulders up, and stretched his arms even wider.

"I want you to leave my friends the hell alone."

Cori squeezed his shoulder. Sam put his hand over hers.

Davenport cleared his throat and sneered.

"I'm afraid I cannot abide by your request." He raised his hands toward Cori and me. I felt icy fingers around my throat, but when I reached to pry them off, there was nothing there. My feet left the ground as I was pulled up off the floor. The "fingers" tightened their hold, and I started to struggle for air.

"No!" Sam said, grabbing my legs and yanking me down. I sputtered, trying to get in as much air as I could, but my throat was gripped too tight. Next to me, Cori was floating like I was, her face brick red. We stared at each other. Her eyes were round and brimming with tears. She mouthed something that looked like *goodbye*. Then her face turned from red to gray, and her eyeballs rolled back until they became completely white, but didn't shut.

"It's a pity you can't help them," Davenport said to Sam, his hands still raised. "But your services are no longer needed."

I realized we were moving, floating closer and closer to the machine. Cori was parallel to me, Sam pulling at her feet with all his might.

"I have so enjoyed our time together," Davenport bellowed. "I really—" He clutched his chest. He staggered a little. His eyes bounced around in panic. "Something is wrong with this body." Davenport fell to his knees. Cori and I fell with him.

I heard her body make a solid thump as she hit the ground. I gasped, sucking in air. Sam rushed to Cori, holding her. She was completely still for a terrible second, and then she started to cough, regaining her normal color. When I could breathe enough to move, I crawled over to my friends.

Davenport gasped. It was the exact same way Rob had sounded on the drive over here.

"The pills," I realized. Cori and Sam looked at me blankly. "Rob took something before the ceremony. He said he was trying to make it right."

Davenport's eyes bulged. He frantically checked his pockets, until he found the bottle. He fumbled, almost dropped it as he brought it to his face and squinted at the label.

"No!" he screamed. "This body is unsafe!" He crawled to the silent machine. "Let me in! I must begin again!"

The machine started up. The music, lights, and the humming and zapping sound effects all filled the portal. The red eyes in the back of the playfield stared down at Davenport in Rob's shell. Its voice loudly declared, "I AM THE MASTER."

An explosion of orange flame burst out of the dragon's mouth, becoming more and more blinding the closer it got to Davenport. The flame didn't burn Davenport but encompassed him, swirling around him like a web, then raised his limp body into the air. I expected it to suck him into the machine. Instead, the flame hurled Davenport into the black void surrounding it. We heard him scream, and then he vanished. The red eyes flashed. "YOU ARE DONE, MORTAL."

"He's gone," Sam whispered.

"Good," Cori said in between coughs, rubbing her neck.

"I mean, he's not in my head anymore," Sam said, turning to us, a smile on his face. "He's *gone* gone."

"Does this mean you can stay?" I asked.

His eyes were hopeful as he raised his head to the ceiling. We watched him in silence.

"I don't hear them screaming." Sam's voice softened. "And I don't feel Nick and the others waking up." He bowed his head and stared at the machine. "So no, I can't stay."

None of us said anything for a while.

"There has to be some other way," I protested.

"I have to go back. The machine might not need offerings anymore now that Davenport is donezo, but it still has me and the others in there. If I don't go back in, everyone I borrowed time from . . . they'll be stuck forever." I started to feel tears creeping down my cheeks. "It'll be okay, Maz."

Cori picked up the spell book. She looked at the page, biting her lip and trying to make it out, but I could tell she didn't know what she was looking at.

"It's not impossible to get you and the others out," Cori said. "We need some time. And some help."

Sam shook his head. "I don't know what we'd come back to. Or what we'd come back *as*. If we'd age or even be human like we were again." Sam stepped toward Cori. "I guess this is it." Sam looked at the START button on the machine. "When I go back, promise me you two won't worry about me."

"How could we not?" I asked.

"I mean it, Maz," Sam said. "I don't want you to beat your-selves up. It wasn't your fault."

He could have said that a million times and I still wouldn't believe him. But I had to. He was making me promise.

"Do you want us to send a message to your dad?" Cori asked.

Sam thought about it for a few moments. "I guess the right thing to do would be to not tell him about all this? We don't know if I'll be able to come out again, so . . ." Sam was quiet for a moment, then said, "Best to let sleeping dogs lie. Oh crap, bad expression!" He winced. "I'm really sorry about Potato Chip. He'll be back soon."

Cori lunged at him, catching him in a bear hug. He stumbled a little.

"I love you, Sam," Cori sobbed, sloppy tears rolling down her face. "Always."

"You better," Sam said. "Maz is going to need you this time around."

She laughed a little through her tears. I did, too. He let go of her and she leaned over and kissed him on his cheek.

"We'll look out for each other," Cori vowed.

Then Sam turned to me and put his hand up for a high five. I stared at it, trying to think of some way to stall for a little more time.

"Don't leave me hanging, Maz," Sam said.

After a few seconds, I slapped his hand, clasping it on impact. We both grunted "Buds" before letting go.

"Promise me something?" Sam asked me, while I wiped at my eyes with my sleeves. "You only get one chance out here. There's only one 'game over.' I don't want you to mope over me or drink a lot like that jerk Paul said you do. I want you to take care of yourself, okay? You're going to have lots more friends, but make sure they're good to you. That they're there for you like you were for me."

I brought him to me for what I knew was one last hug. I held on, thinking about all the milestones he'd never see, all the memories we shared, how every friend I made for the rest of my life wouldn't know him.

He was the first to let go.

He turned and walked over to the machine. It began to hum. Three balls rolled out of a ramp and locked into place behind the plunger spring. The START button lit up.

Sam looked over his shoulder at us, a small smile on his face. Then he pushed the button. A blinding light filled the room. When my vision cleared, Sam was gone.

"Maz?" Cori called to me.

I went to her and held her shoulders. "I'm here," I said.

She blinked until she could see me, her eyes filled with tears. She looked at the sleeping machine. The wall was back to normal, with no portal of darkness in sight.

"He's gone," Cori said as she turned to me. We both kept crying, and we held on to each other until Brooks and Tiffany came down the stairs.

"What the hell is going on?" Tiffany asked Cori. We turned to look at them. Tiffany's hair was mussed; she had suitcases under her eyes instead of bags and looked wearier than someone her age should. She wore a yellow satin teddy underneath a half-opened robe in the same color. When she saw me, she tightened the belt of her robe. "Maz?" she asked.

"Hi, Tiffany. Nice digs," I said. I couldn't bring myself to let go of Cori. Brooks was in Joe Boxer shorts, his bare legs exposed. His hairline was receding already, and his stomach was a little rounder than it was in the wedding photo I saw at Cori's house. He still had shaving cream on his cheeks and around his mouth. He looked like a Santa with a shaving cream beard.

"Are you two okay?" Cori asked them.

"Yeah, but I had the weirdest dream," Brooks said. "I thought I saw that missing kid you used to be friends with in my bathroom."

"Better Sam Bennett than that plain Jane in accounting who is always sniffing around you," Tiffany muttered.

"For the last time, she is only a colleague," Brooks insisted.

"Yeah, they're okay," Cori said to me, laughing through her tears.

38.

THERE WERE A FEW UNUSUAL THINGS that happened after Sam's second disappearance. The first were news reports of missing pets being found by their owners, alive and well, including Potato Chip, who had relieved himself in Tiffany's closet. I had never been happier to clean up dog pee. Inside animal control trucks and veterinary clinics, the wildlife that had been frozen on the Carter Prep track sprang back into action.

The second was that, like Brooks and Tiffany, Nick and a movie theater employee woke up from a deep sleep.

And the third unusual thing . . .

"Your 1992–1993 homecoming queen is . . ." Vickie said into the microphone. The gym buzzed with excitement as Vickie opened the envelope. She grinned and rolled her eyes as soon as she read the notecard. "Corinne O'Brien!"

"Shoot me now," I said to my date over the roar of applause. We were both still grieving, but it had given us a little boost to see each other dressed up for a dance.

"Your subjects need you," Maz said as he clapped for me. He was dressed in a tux, looking incredibly dapper, and taking his date duties very seriously.

I walked toward the stage in a black dress that Tiffany had bought me. The crowd parted for me, applauding for the person they thought I was. Nick was already onstage wearing his crown. He clapped halfheartedly.

"Congratulations," Vickie said as she lifted my tiara, motioning for me to duck down. I did, and Vickie placed a silly piece of plastic on my perfectly coiffed head. I had prepared a short speech, something about school spirit and how we should have the best senior year ever. All the words I thought I'd say left my brain as soon as I saw Janet walk into the room. She wore a purple dress, combat boots, a white corsage, and a smile directed right at me.

I didn't realize how long I was standing onstage without saying anything until Vickie nudged me from behind. Then I began.

"These traditions, these events, they're all ways to remember our time in high school. We'll look back at our yearbooks and maybe remember who won Most Likely to Succeed or Best Dressed. Superlatives given to us by our peers based on what they think they know about us."

I stopped for a moment, wondering what Sam would think of this. He'd be making funny faces at me from the crowd, trying to get me to crack up.

"A lot of this time in our lives is about how we'll be remembered. What I'd really like to be remembered for is being a good, genuine friend. I know I haven't always lived up to that. So, in this, our final year of high school, let's try and be the best friends to one another that we can be. Thank you."

Then Vickie announced the homecoming queen and king would share a dance. Nick guided me to the center of the floor.

"You look beautiful," he said as we awkwardly swayed together. "So Maz, huh?"

"He's my friend."

"That's all?"

I snuck a glance at Janet. She'd dyed her hair back to black and pulled it up halfway. She was so ridiculously gorgeous. "That's all." I imagined what Nick's face would look like at our tenth reunion when I showed up with a date I really wanted. Hopefully I'd be brave enough by then. "Besides, you won't have any shortage of dates now that you're king."

He grinned a little, his ego somewhat healed. When the song ended, he bowed gallantly and I rolled my eyes as I curtsied. The Nick and Cori show was officially, and amicably, over.

Vickie swooped in. I assumed she was about to pounce on Nick, but she slid her arm through mine instead. "Nice speech."

"You would have made a better one," I replied.

She squeezed me closer to her. "Most likely. Hi, Janet," Vickie said, giving her a tentative wave. "I love your dress."

"Hey. I love yours, too," Janet said.

I was still getting used to them talking to each other. We had yet to do a proper girls' hang, but I would try to think of something all of us could enjoy.

"Congratulations, Your Royal Highness," Maz said, giving me a golf clap. "Hi, Vickie. You look exquisite, as does this soiree."

"I sure do," Vickie replied with a laugh, a little color blooming in her cheeks. "I was wondering if you'd want to dance? If that's okay with your date?"

Janet and I looked at each other in surprise.

"It's fine with me," I said. "Is it fine with you, Maz?"

Maz straightened his bowtie, offered his arm to Vickie, and the two walked onto the dance floor.

I looked at Janet, trying not to stare. "I didn't think you'd be here."

"I didn't think I'd be here either," she said with a shrug. "But someone did drop off a corsage for me, just in case."

"I'm glad it got to you."

"Well, Maz also called me. He said if I didn't have a date, he would be happy to enlist a respectful gentleman."

"He did?" I watched Maz get down. A crowd was forming around him and Vickie, clapping as he twirled her around. Guess some of Sam's moves had rubbed off on him.

"He's a surprisingly persuasive guy. He really thinks the world of you."

"As a friend," I clarified quickly.

"Yes, Cori. As a *friend*, I know," Janet said, a little bit of a laugh in her voice. "How are you feeling?"

"I miss him," I said. She rubbed my arm. She was close enough that she could see my eyes flick to her lips. "You have any after-dance plans?"

"Depends," she said, her voice soft and sweet. "What did you have in mind?"

"Spending time with you."

She leaned forward, kissed me on my cheek at the corner of my lips.

"I do have an episode of *Tales from the Crypt* I haven't watched yet," she said. "To be clear, there will be breaks for—"

"Yes!" I said. "Always breaks for that."

We both laughed.

"Congratulations, Queen Cori."

39

MAZ

I WASN'T SURE IF I SHOULD SAY ANYTHING about Cori's new look. She hadn't mentioned anything about it over the phone. We talked once a week. I thought that would change once we got settled at school, but like clockwork, she called every Sunday afternoon at five o'clock.

"You don't like it?" Cori asked as she walked toward me.

"Like what?" I pretended to be oblivious.

"My hair," she said, giving me a hug.

"I went longer, you went shorter. I think it works, no?"

"Yeah, but it's also green."

"It's a bold choice for a bold woman," I said with a grin.

She pulled on one of my curls. "You ready?"

"Oh, I almost forgot." I leaned back into my car and grabbed a box of chocolates. "I got her the caramel turtles. She liked them last time."

We walked up the brick stairs to the Davenport estate. Lizzy had been renovating it, and it looked friendlier, more like a home, and less like a creepy hideout for an evil recluse.

"It's temporary. The color," Cori said when we reached the front door. "But I'm kind of into it."

"I bet Janet is, too," I said, ringing the doorbell.

She didn't talk to me much about their relationship, but she did tell me they were giving long distance a try. Janet was studying at Oberlin. Cori was at NYU, thanks to Brooks and Tiffany.

"Speaking of which," she said. "We're going to a party at Vickie's for a little bit. Pre-Thanksgiving reunion bash. She'd *love* for you to be there."

Vickie and I had shared a few romantic moments after the dance last year, but both agreed that when we started college, we should be single. I was having fun at Bates, but not partying as much as I used to. Who picks freshman year of college to cut back on drinking? I still knew how to have a good time, though. I was meeting lots of new, cool people. And I liked being close enough to home that it wasn't a big deal to check in. I was glad to see that Nilou and Cleo had become good friends. And I had visited Vickie at Bentley a few times. I liked being around her. I could be myself because she knew everything.

"Is it cool if I bring Derek? He's back from Columbia."

"Of course! Also, tell your mom I'm bringing pumpkin pie for dessert on Thursday after I do dinner at my place."

Lizzy opened the door. "Hello!" She wrapped one arm around each of us and hugged us both at the same time. "I've missed you! Come in, you need to tell me about your adventures!"

We stepped inside, the sweet smell of baked goods floating in the air.

"I've made corn muffins." Then she spotted the box of chocolates in my hand and said, "Oh, Maziyar, you didn't have to. But I'm glad you did. I want to show you something."

She headed straight up the grand bifurcated staircase, and we followed her. We walked down a freshly painted hallway, and she opened a door for us. Inside was a fully furnished bedroom for a twelve-year-old boy. A very specific twelve-year-old boy.

"Do you think he'll like it?" Lizzy asked.

I took a step inside. There was not only a giant TV in his room, but also a VCR, a Sega Genesis, and a Super Nintendo. There were posters of his favorite wrestlers, including the Iron Sheik (who I had mixed feelings about), and "Macho Man" Randy Savage snapping into a Slim Jim. On the bookshelf, alongside plenty of comics and VHS tapes, was a framed photograph of the three of us. I remembered the day it was taken. We were in first grade, sitting at the kitchen table in my old apartment, dyeing eggs for our family's Nowruz display. Sam held an egg to his open mouth, pretending like he was going to take a bite out of it. Cori was missing some teeth, so her mouth was closed when she was supposed to say "Cheese." I held my purple egg up with pride, beaming at the camera.

"He's going to love it," I said.

"This is really generous," Cori agreed. After Rob was declared dead, Ms. Davenport had inherited her uncle's estate. Mr. Davenport's agreement with Rob had been a temporary one, so with both of them gone, Lizzy had been given reign over Davenport enterprises. "May we see him?"

"Of course!" she said cheerily. We all exited Sam's bedroom.

"I've been making real progress. I'm sorry I haven't figured it out yet. But I'm closer."

She pulled the door to the attic down from the ceiling, unfolding the ladder. Maz and I thanked her and climbed up.

The *Sorcerer* machine stood in the center of the room, surrounded by cardboard storage boxes and random household items that were no longer of use. As always, it was unplugged. Cori and I stepped closer to it, both of us putting a hand on the playfield glass.

"Hi, Sam," Cori said. "It's us."

The machine came alive, its sound effects trilling and all its colorful lights twinkling in rapid succession.

"We're going to get you out, bud," I said. I felt it, too. It was only a matter of time.

The red eyes that stared out from the game no longer terrified me. I knew Sam was somewhere behind them.

GAME OVER.

PLAY AGAIN?

ACKNOWLEDGMENTS

This story has been a dream project for me, and writing it during a global pandemic served as a wonderful escape. I am forever grateful to the following people for letting me spend time in the escape hatch: Elise Howard, one of the best editors in the world and a wonderful person who changed my life. Thank you for taking a chance on me. If you ever need anything, I am there. Susan Ginsburg, my agent extraordinaire, who heard me pitch a story about a pinball machine that eats people and said it sounded good! Thank you for always being there for me and taking care of business. Catherine Bradshaw, you are a treasure; thank you for always emailing me back. Sarah Alpert, this book would not be possible without you. Thank you for your patience, your hard work, your understanding, and for seeing the vision of this story and its characters when it wasn't always apparent. You are an incredible talent.

Caitlin Rubinstein, for always being so supportive. Ashley Mason and Janice Lee and all the proofreaders, for going through the story with fine-toothed combs and *really* saving the day regarding timeline errors. Michael McKenzie, Shaelyn McDaniel, Diana Griffin, Adah Li, Annie Mazes, Ilana Gold, Laura Essex, and everyone past and present in the Algonquin Young Readers crew. Colin Verdi, for one of the best covers in the world! I am a fan of yours for life. To the *Dead Flip* audiobook cast, Wali Habib, Reena Dutt, and Michael Crouch, thank you for bringing the characters to life.

Mom, I am so proud of you: thank you for always being such a believer in me and my stories. I believe in you and I love you more than Prince songs, *Gremlins*, and *Pee Wee's Playhouse*, which, as you know, is A LOT of love. Dad, you are so wonderful: thank you for your support. I love when you ask me "Did you finish your book?" and I can reply "Which one?" and we both laugh. Donna, thank you for reading an early draft and not getting too annoyed when I kept watching you to see what you thought. Thanks also for giving me some of the best Halloween memories. Ashi, Kian, and Shahab, thank you for being a source of constant support and for dropping off soup. Rana, thank you for going on walks with me and watching *The Karate Kid*, *The Lost Boys*, and *The Monster Squad* even when they are not your jam.

Maria Reyes, for watching almost every episode of *The Twilight Zone* with me. Olivia Klein and Emma Mouradian, for traveling with me to Free Play in Rhode Island to play and research a genuine *Sorcerer* pinball machine. Kia, Antonia, Bailey, Stephanie, Corinne, and Leila: you'll never know how much our talks mean to me. Laura Kinney, because you've heard it all. Josh, Melody, Carolina, Autumn, Marnie, Kate, Savannah, Andrea, Kaveh, Jacqui, Rachel, Benielle, Paul and Jenn, Hilary, Gaby, Keegan and Lindsay, Brette, Kevin, Eric, Sumit, Pavani, and Jess and Jordan, for checking in and talking and being good people. Author friends who checked in during the pandemic just to say hey: it means so much because I never want to bother any of you (ha-ha). In particular, Sara Saedi, Adib Khorram, Kelly Quindlen, Aminah Mae Safi, Lamar Giles, Maggie Tokuda-Hall, Nic Stone,

Rebecca Kim Wells, Ryan La Sala, Katie Cotugno, Tracey Baptiste, Cynthia Platt, Marjan Kamali, Malinda Lo, Zack Clark, and especially David Levithan, for writing me letters. Chris Lynch, you are a legend. Natasha, thank you for being a friend like any true Golden Girl would be. You bring me joy and I hope I do the same for you. You'll have me saying "marshmallow" forever. Meredith Goldstein, you are one of the best friends I'll ever have. I hope I give you even a fraction of the fun and peace that you bring me. I can never thank you enough.

The cast and crew of *Svengoolie* and *Toon in with Me*: thank you for helping to pass the time and letting me know what day it was. The crew at Paddle Boston, for helping me get into kayaks. Steve at Outer Limits, for letting me hang out at the best shop around. David and Elizabeth Lepie, for being the best trick-or-treating crew a kid could ask for. Thank you to Waban News, for being my first comic book store, and the late Bob Smith, who sold the best candy and would never have a nefarious pinball machine in his store. Thank you to the Williams Company for creating such a creepy pinball machine that was a great inspiration. Thank you to every teacher I've ever had.

Thank you to reviewers, bloggers, librarians, teachers, professors, booksellers, podcasters, social media folks, freelancers, journalists, media outlets, students, and everyone who has given my work a chance and has spread the word: I thank you forever and always and feel so grateful for your support and time.

And most important of all, thank you, dear reader, for spending time with Cori, Maz, and Sam. I loved spending time with them and I hope you did, too. This was a story about outgrowing friendships, how nostalgia can be fun but also deceptive, and how love is everlasting even when we think it isn't. Thank you for letting me tell this story and for deciding to pick it up. I hope it inspires you to read more stories and to write the story of your dreams.